"Are you serious about Ellis?"

Bill Robichaux's question caught Autumn off guard.

"Ellis? No, of course not," she said hastily.

"Well, he's serious about you. Do you think it's fair to encourage him if you don't feel the same way?" At her inquiring look, he grated out, "Don't look so innocent! There must have been plenty already. Do you keep a record of how many men fall in love with you?"

"Don't be any more obnoxious than you can help!" Autumn hissed. "I'm glad of my date with Ellis, otherwise I might have gone out with you!"

His eyes glinted. "You didn't consider me so unacceptable last night," he reminded her. "My kisses then—today, Ellis's. Do you tally them up, too?"

Bellefleur

by

SONDRA STANFORD

Harlequin Books

TORONTO • LONDON • LOS ANGELES • AMSTERDAM
SYDNEY • HAMBURG • PARIS • STOCKHOLM • ATHENS • TOKYO

Original hardcover edition published in 1980
by Mills & Boon Limited

ISBN 0-373-02354-5

Harlequin edition published September 1980

CHAPTER ONE

SOME forty-odd miles roughly south-west of New Orleans, it happened. Autumn McBride's shapely foot pressed the car's brakes gently, then she carefully manoeuvred the green Datsun on to the grassy shoulder of the road and cut the motor.

She sighed deeply, opened the car door and stepped out. An instant later her worst fears were confirmed. The left back tire was flat. Worse still, she didn't have the first notion about how to go about changing it.

She gazed longingly at the road as though by magic she might conjure up a passing motorist with a good heart and a vast experience at tire-changing. But the road remained obstinately empty.

A short distance ahead, the country road became a bridge over a bayou, and picking up again on the opposite bank, it then disappeared behind huge oaks draped with straggling grey Spanish moss. Behind her and on each side of the road, the scenery was the same. The only sound was the high-pitched hum of insects. It was almost eerie how foreign and mysterious the place seemed—a far, far cry from bustling New York.

Well, get to it, she chided herself. With a rueful glance down at her spotless white pants suit, she reached into the car, pulled out the keys and walked towards the back. She would get out the spare tire and the jack and pray she could figure out what to do by herself. *You would think,* she angrily told herself, *that by the time a girl reaches the age of twenty-three in these enlightened times, she would be knowledgeable and experienced about tires and car motors and other related subjects!* Instead, she felt about as helpless as a three-year-old.

It was then that she noticed the truck. It was parked a few yards back and was partially concealed from the road by a screen of wild cane and tall weeds. She supposed that was how she had managed to pass it by without seeing it. It was black, old and dilapidated, and she supposed it had been abandoned. No help there.

She turned back to the car, about to open the trunk, when she noticed a movement out of the corner of her eye. A man was approaching from the direction of the bayou. In one hand he was carrying a stringer of catfish; in the other, a fishing rod. He was dressed in disreputable baggy brown pants with a hole in one of the knees, a green and white plaid shirt that was half tucked in, half dangling, and he wore a black cap above a face that appeared dark, how much from dirt, how much from nature, Autumn couldn't tell.

As the man came forward, a shudder ran up her spine. She was only too acutely conscious of her position, a lone female on a deserted road. She stood very straight and still, holding her breath and knotting her hands nervously at her sides as the man neared her.

He was even with her now, towering a good eight inches above her, and she was no midget herself at five feet eight. She could see clearly his midnight-dark eyes, his thick brows, the strong lines of mouth and chin; rock-hard shoulders stretched the fabric of his shirt taut; strong yet curiously graceful hands gripped rod and stringer. He looked to be in his mid-thirties, a specimen of arrogant, virile manhood. Would he attempt to harm her? And if he did, would she stand a chance of getting free of him? Of being able to run for help?

The man was looking at her closely now. His bold gaze lingered on her face as though taking in every detail of gold-flecked brown eyes, thick dark lashes, vulnerable soft, pink lips, before it travelled down her body, slowly taking in every curving detail of it as well. Autumn itched to slap him as her skin burned with uneasy self-consciousness. His gaze sought her face again and this time there was a slight twitch to his lips, as though he found something amusing about her body. Then the moment passed and so did the man. Without even breaking his gait or so much as nodding to her, he walked right on by.

For a long moment Autumn was too frozen with shock even to realise what had happened. When she did, and managed to turn to look after him, the man had almost reached the black truck. He not only had not bothered or attempted to harm her, but he had also rudely ignored her obvious need for help. And regardless of what she privately thought about him, she still needed that tire changed.

Gathering up her shredded courage, she called out in a dry, scratchy throat, 'Ex ... excuse me. Can you please help me?'

The man slightly turned so that he was looking at her over his shoulder. 'Did you want something?' he asked in a very cool, unapproachable voice.

'Damn you!' she thought furiously. Aloud, she managed meekly, 'Can...can you please help me? I...I've got a flat tire.'

He just looked at her for another instant, wordlessly, then turned and resumed his way to the truck.

'Well, of all the rude ...!' Autumn muttered beneath her breath. She whirled round and shoved the key into the lock of the trunk with some difficulty, since by now she was shaking with anger. But finally she had it open and with one last sigh for the expensive white pants suit she wore, she reached towards the back for the spare tire.

Strong brown hands suddenly covered hers. 'If you'll move out of the way,' the voice suggested calmly, 'I'll get it out.'

She looked up to find the man beside her. Suddenly she was aware that his hands still rested on hers. With a convulsive jerk she withdrew her hands from the tire and backed a step away. 'You...you didn't answer me when I asked you for help, so naturally I assumed you didn't intend to do it.'

The look he cast her was one of scarcely concealed amusement. 'You wouldn't have wanted me to ask you to hold my stringer of fish, would you?'

Autumn's face flinched. 'No, of course not.'

'I thought not. That's why I went on to the truck – to deposit the fish there.' The man spoke as though he was explaining something to a child.

'Oh,' said Autumn, feeling inadequate and completely out of her depth.

With quick, experienced movements, he had the spare out of the trunk and on to the ground and the jack cranking up the back of the car. 'Is ... is there anything I can do to help?' Autumn offered shyly as she stood to one side.

'No, ma'am,' he answered. His tone was deliberately patient. 'Besides, you might get that pretty outfit dirty.' His eyes met hers for a brief instant.

'Where are you headed?' he asked now, as he worked. 'You're on a very little used road.'

'I'm going to St Pierre,' she answered. 'The map showed this road to be a bit of a short cut from New Orleans.'

'St Pierre, hm? Where are you from?'

'New York.' She glanced down the road. 'Can you tell me how much further it is?'

Now he had the old tire off and was putting the spare on.

'About seven miles,' he said. 'You going to stay with relatives there?'

'No, she answered shortly. She really didn't feel like discussing her private business with a total stranger on the side of a road, so she hoped her abruptness might curb his curiosity.

It didn't. 'A boarding house? There are no motels there, you know. Haven't ever needed any—tourists don't visit St Pierre. Does Mrs Theriot know you're coming? Sometimes, if she's down in her back, she won't take in boarders.'

'I'm *not* staying at a boarding house,' she was goaded into admitting.

'No?' He looked at her with a definite question in both

his voice and his eyes and he was seemingly oblivious of her obvious exasperation. 'Then where are you planning to stay?'

'I've inherited a house there,' she said finally, blurting out the truth.

'Is that so?' His jaw suddenly turned rock-hard with a strange tenseness. But the next moment Autumn decided she had imagined it. He stood up now, finished with the tire, and rubbed his chin thoughtfully. 'Now that'd be Miss Hattie's place, wouldn't it?' he asked mildly.

'It would,' she admitted through gritted teeth. She went over and opened the car door and pulled out her purse. A moment later, as the man had finished stowing the jack and the flat tire into the trunk, she handed him a folded green bill. 'Thank you so much for helping me out.'

He looked at the money in her hand and then at her. There was an odd expression in his eyes that she couldn't understand. 'Please,' she urged as she held the bill closer to him, 'please take it. I'd like to show you my appreciation for your help.'

Slowly he reached out a hand and took the five dollars from her. He unfolded the bill with both hands and stood looking at it for a long moment. Autumn felt embarrassed. She always did whenever a tip was called for. She was never sure whether she had given too much or not enough—or whether it should have been offered at all.

Now the man was folding it neatly and a moment later he dropped it into his pocket. Raising his hand, he tipped his cap politely at her. 'Thank you, ma'am,' he said with such politeness that she at once sensed a falseness about it. Then he turned and walked swiftly away to his truck.

Autumn crawled into the car and started the motor, vastly relieved to have the tire changed and also to get away from that disturbing man.

A moment later his black truck pulled on to the road and with a jaunty wave of his hand, he was gone. Autumn slumped in the seat, trying to relax a moment, but instead she felt as taut as a violin string. She looked at her face in the rear-view mirror. What was there that the man had seen about her that was so amusing? Did she have a smudge or something? But the mirror put to rest that worry and after a moment her face puckered into a thoughtful frown. She looked just the same as always; her long, auburn hair was neat against her shoulders, her make-up was faultless, accenting her soft brown eyes and her high cheekbones, and her lipstick wasn't smeared, so what was it?

She shrugged impatiently. Why let the man bother her? He was just a bum, judging by his clothes and his truck. Probably an illiterate trapper or fisherman down on his luck. Yet she had been aware of eyes that held a keen, lively intelligence, and there had been a certain strength and dignity to the chin. His firm mouth had a definite hint of command.

Autumn shrugged again, turning the steering wheel to the left and pulling out on to the road. She would simply dismiss the man and his derisive airs from her mind. Certainly he wasn't worthy of a second thought.

A few minutes later she was entering St Pierre. She slowed her speed so that she had time to glance around. There was no sign of the black truck which had preceded her. She was glad that she needn't see the man again today. What she needed to do now was to find someone who could direct her to the offices of Naquin and Naquin.

St Pierre was a small community, its streets heavily shaded by sprawling branches of live oaks, which wore shawls of moss. Though in actual fact it was a blazing hot August afternoon, the town looked cool and untouched by the heavy, humid heat.

She stopped at a service station for gasoline and the operator readily explained how she could find the Naquin lawyers' offices. A short time later as she drove towards their offices, she shook her head in disbelief. It still all seemed like a dream—giving up her life as a successful model in New York in order to come here to live in a house she had inherited from a comparative stranger. Joyce, her room-mate in New York, had flatly told her she was crazy even to think of burying herself in the swamps of southern Louisiana, but somehow Autumn felt it was the right thing to do. Especially since she had needed to get completely away from Don Prescott, or even the memory of him.

Now she blew a kiss heavenward. 'Thanks, Miss Hattie,' she whispered. 'Wherever you are.'

Two years ago when she had met Miss Hattie, the last thing on her mind had been houses, least of all houses in Louisiana. They had met on a cold, grey day on a Man-hattan street. And 'met' could hardly be the correct word to use. 'Encountered' was better. Miss Hattie Robi-chaux, a tourist on her first and only visit to the big city, a tiny grey-haired lady, was valiantly trying to fight off a fierce mugger who had jumped out of an alleyway and begun attacking her. Autumn was a few yards away when she first noticed what was going on—noticed, too, that two or three men pedestrians had simply walked on past rather than stopping to help. Born and bred in New York, Autumn knew a person was better off not to get involved in things that weren't strictly her business, but this was one time she couldn't ignore what was happening. The sight of that tiny little woman courageously fighting for her life beneath the brutal onslaughts of the husky mugger was too much. She waded in, slinging at the mugger with her handbag. When the strap broke on that, she dropped it to the ground and began clawing at him with her long fingernails, yelling at him to pick on somebody his own size.

She chuckled, remembering the mugger's words. 'What, are ya crazy, lady?' He had broken away from her and fled, forgetful of the little lady's purse he had intended to snatch, eager only to get free of sharp, dangerous fingernails. Autumn had then screamed at a passerby to fetch a police-man and an ambulance as she jerked off her own coat and spread it over the small, still body which now lay uncon-scious on the sidewalk.

When the ambulance came she went with it to the hospital and for the next few days she had cheerfully visited Miss Hattie daily. They had made fast friends and Miss Hattie hadn't been able to thank Autumn enough for saving her life. But when she left town and had gone back home to Louisiana, Autumn had all but forgotten the incident and the lady except at Christmas time when they exchanged cards.

Until three weeks ago when she had received a letter from a lawyer advising her that Miss Hattie had died and left her a house just at a time when she was most ready for a big change in her life.

But she clamped a lid on that thought. She had lawyers to see just now. She had no time to spare a thought for Don and the way he had hurt her.

Twenty minutes later she was staring at the grey-haired, middle-aged lawyer with disbelief. 'Let me get this straight,' she gasped. 'According to you, I am now the owner of a plantation house?'

Mr Naquin nodded. 'It's called Bellefleur.'

Beautiful flower. It was a wonderful name for a home, but at the moment Autumn was in no position to admire it. 'Yet I'm not free,' she enquired insistently, 'to either sell it or to displace the present occupants? Is that correct?'

'More or less,' the lawyer agreed. He leaned back in his chair and adjusted his eyeglasses upon his nose. 'As I've already explained, Dr Robichaux is Miss Robichaux's nephew. She has willed to him all the estate agricultural property, which comprises the sugar cane and soybean fields surrounding the house, but she has left you the house itself. However, his medical offices are situated in one wing of the house and he's lived in the main part of it since he was just a boy. Miss Robichaux merely wanted to make certain that he would not be displaced—or his medical practice. Unless he himself wishes to move out, of course. And also she asks that you give a home to her housekeeper and friend of many years, Mrs Bertha Guidry. It's also true that you can't sell the house for five years and that then you must give Dr Robichaux first refusal, but after that you would be free to sell it on the open market.'

Autumn shook her head. 'I don't understand why she didn't just go ahead and will the house to Dr Robichaux in the first place.'

The expression on the lawyer's face told her plainly that he didn't understand it, either, though he attempted to explain it. 'She was grateful to you for saving her life, Miss McBride. It was the only way she could think of to show it.'

'Am I allowed to live in the house myself?'

He looked surprised. 'Of course you are. The will merely states that you can't sell it for five years or remove the present occupants before then. But there's plenty of room there for the three of you.' He looked uncertain for a moment. 'Do you have family members who are coming to reside with you at Bellefleur?'

Autumn smiled and shook her head. 'No, just myself. Well, Mr Naquin, if you could just direct me as to how I can get to Bellefleur?'

Before he could answer, there came a soft knock at the door, followed by its opening. 'Dad, there's something I need to discuss ...' The young man who had entered looked up from the papers he carried in his hands, and when he saw Autumn, he halted. 'Oh, excuse me,' he apologised. 'I didn't know you had anyone with you.' He turned to leave.

Mr Naquin halted him. 'Wait—don't go. Miss McBride, I'd like you to meet my son, Ellis. Ellis, Miss Autumn McBride.'

Ellis Naquin had handsome, even features that became downright engaging when he smiled. His dark eyes were warm as he held out a hand to Autumn and said, 'I'm pleased to meet you. Now, haven't I heard your name some place before?'

'Miss McBride has come to claim Bellefleur Plantation, Ellis. In fact, I was just about to give her its direction.'

Enlightenment dawned. 'Oh, *that* Miss McBride.' He looked at his father. 'But did we know Miss McBride was arriving today, sir?'

Mr Naquin smiled and shook his head. 'No, we didn't. I'm as much surprised as you.'

The younger man returned his gaze to Autumn. 'Then that means you're not expected at Bellefleur today.'

Autumn shook her head. 'Of course not. Until a half hour ago, I didn't realise there was anyone there to advise of my coming. Your father has just finished explaining about a Dr Robichaux and a housekeeper, a Mrs Guidry, I believe, who are living there.'

Ellis smiled and nodded. 'Right. Have you seen the place yet?'

'No. Your father was just about to give me directions on how I could get there.'

'No need,' said Ellis. 'I'll go with you out there ... introduce you to Mrs Guidry and Dr Robichaux if you like.'

'Will you?' Autumn asked with relief flooding her voice. She smiled her thanks. 'I'd appreciate it so much. I rather dreaded going all alone.'

The elder Mr Naquin gave her a key to the house which he had been holding for her, shook her hand and bade her goodbye as Ellis, his hand on her elbow, ushered her out of the door.

'Could I talk you into having a drink with me before we go out there?' he asked as they emerged from the building into the heavy heat of the day.

'No, thanks,' she said. 'I'd really like to get to the house.'

Ellis Naquin sighed. 'Just my luck—a beautiful new girl arrives in town and she's more interested in an old plantation house than she is in me!'

Autumn laughed. 'Sorry, but I'm afraid you're right. Your father's letter never said I was inheriting a plantation house. I can't wait to see it!'

'Well, let's get on with it, then. Maybe in a few days, you'll be bored enough to want to go out with me after all.'

'Maybe I will,' Autumn agreed. Then, appalled, she realised what a trap she had fallen into. 'I didn't mean I'd be *bored*,' she began.

But Ellis only laughed. 'I asked for it,' he admitted.

Autumn got into the Datsun and followed Ellis, who drove his Chrysler, down the street. She decided she liked him. He was open and friendly, even flirtatious, a far cry from her imagined idea of a stuffed-shirt lawyer. But, and now her mouth pursed grimly, she was not going to get interested in any man, no matter how appealing. Don had cured her of that.

She had met Don Prescott about three months ago at a cocktail party in Manhattan. Joyce, her apartment mate, was always dragging her to parties ever since she had talked Autumn into giving up her secretarial job and going into modelling. 'A model needs to be seen, noticed,' she'd insisted. And at the right parties, one was seen and noticed. And Don had been at one of them, an up-and-coming young stockbroker on Wall Street.

They had dated only occasionally at first, but soon the friendship had ripened into love. The rift with Don had occurred because Autumn was old-fashioned despite her rather sophisticated looks. To her, love meant marriage. To Don it meant having an affair and living together. She had found that out a month ago when Joyce had suddenly announced that she was about to marry. Autumn was worried about getting a new apartment mate to share the rent and that was when Don had suggested they live together. But when she asked if he meant marriage, he had laughed. 'We're not ready for that yet, baby. Why, we've only known each other a few months. But if we live together, we'll find out if we're really suited or not.' When she had refused, Don had angrily told her that if she didn't comply, he knew another girl who would be happy to move in with him. The upshot was that Autumn had refused to see or even speak to Don again. And when a few days later the letter had arrived advising her of her inheritance in Louisiana, it had seemed like a godsend.

Joyce had argued. 'You're throwing away a successful future because of that bum, Autumn. You'll be the best known model in town in another year if you stick with it. You can't just drop everything and run away just because one guy hurt you.'

But it had been more than that, actually. For one thing, Autumn was tired of the rat race of New York. She had lived there all her life and all the hustle and bustle had never really appealed to her. Her father, when she had been small, had talked of growing up on a farm and of how he wanted to save enough money to buy one. But he had died before he could realise his romantic dream and her mother had had all she could do to support the two of them in the city. Then two years ago her mother had died, and a few months later she had moved into an apartment with Joyce. But now Joyce was about to marry and Autumn, with her parents both gone, no longer had firm ties to New York City. She wanted to see a different part of the country, how people lived in other places, and this seemed a good time to cut the strings and find out.

But the thought of Don still hurt. She had believed that he really loved her and that they were headed towards a life together. Instead she had discovered that he was just a shallow, immature person bent on his own selfish pleasures to the exclusion of a responsible relationship.

She brought her thoughts back to the present and saw Ellis Naquin put on his red indicator light, showing that he was about to turn left. Autumn did the same. The two automobiles rattled on to a narrow wooden bridge over a muddy water hyacinth-choked bayou.

The road, once across the bayou, snaked between rows of stately oaks. The overhanging Spanish moss dripped from their branches almost to the ground in places. Now she could see that the road was actually a drive and that it swept into an arc in front of an enormous old plantation house.

Autumn gasped in delighted amazement. This couldn't be Bellefleur, *her* home now! It was too incredible to believe!

The house was of grand proportions. There was a large two-storied main section, fronted by elegant Ionic columns. A veranda, cooled by late afternoon shadows, stretched along the length of the house and above it was a gallery that was reached from the upstairs bedroom. It was bordered by a delicately designed wooden balustrade. On either end of the main house were identical wings, one storey in height. All windows and doors were shuttered in green, a graceful contrast to the snowy white of the building. Near the house on the front lawn stood a majestic magnolia tree with its delicate, perfumed scent. Beside each wing of the house were pink-flowering crêpe myrtles providing bold splashes of colour.

'Well, what do you think?' Ellis Naquin asked as, now that their cars were parked in the drive, he came to open her car door for her.

'It's incredible!' Autumn breathed. 'I never expected anything quite so big ... or so elegant. How old is it?'

Ellis shook his head. 'Search me,' he told her. 'All I do know for sure is that it was here before the Civil War, because Union Soldiers occupied it and used it for headquarters for a while. Come on,' he added as he swept a hand towards the house. 'Let's go inside.'

When they reached the veranda, Ellis pushed the doorbell while Autumn looked back at the surrounding lawn, across which the setting sun was sending lacy dark shadows cast by the trees. After a few moments Ellis murmured, 'There doesn't seem to be anyone home. I knew the Doc wouldn't be home ... Thursday afternoons he's off. I suppose Mrs Guidry's gone to town for something. Shall we go on inside? Dad gave you a key.'

Autumn frowned. 'I suppose so,' she said doubtfully. 'But I hate just walking in like this ... especially since I'm not expected. But I can't sit out front all afternoon, can I? Do you think they'll mind?'

'Of course not,' Ellis said decisively. 'Besides, it's your house now. How can they mind?' He inserted the key into the lock and pushed open the door.

Autumn stepped into a wide entrance hall with highly polished wooden floors. A stairway at the back of the hall curved gracefully upwards. On either side of the hall were a number of doors. Ellis opened one on the left.

'Anybody home?' Autumn peered into the room past his shoulder. Apparently it was the living room, or rather an old-fashioned parlour. There was a rose velvet love seat with finger-roll carving and a number of chairs and tables, all belonging to roughly the same period. A chandelier hung from the ceiling and the floor was covered by a delicate, beautiful Aubusson carpet.

Ellis pulled the faux bois finished door closed and opened the next one. Here was obviously the library, for its walls were lined with books. This room boasted no antiques except for a lovely library table, but instead, comfortable-looking tan leather sofas and chairs and numerous efficient modern lamps. 'Nobody here, either.'

Autumn was beginning to feel nervous like the trespasser she was. 'Maybe we ought to leave, Ellis. I can come back later. I don't feel right being here.'

'Don't be silly,' he chided her. 'It's your house. Come on, we'll check the kitchen.'

But though they glanced into the formal dining room with its English rosewood table and the old-fashioned kitchen behind it, they found no one.

Ellis was frowning as he glanced at his watch. 'For all I offered you a drink a while earlier, Autumn, I forgot an important appointment. If I leave now, I'll still be able to make it. But I hate to leave you here alone and there's no place for you to go just now on a moment's notice.'

'I'll be all right,' she assured him quickly.

'What will you do?'

'I'll take my suitcases upstairs and settle into one of the bedrooms. By the time I finish, surely someone will be home.'

'I'll bring your suitcases in for you before I go,' he offered.

Autumn shook her head. 'Thanks, but I can get them myself. You're already late enough for your appointment because of me. Thanks very much for bringing me out here.'

Ellis nodded and grinned. 'I'll be seeing you soon, then.'

After he was gone, Autumn went outside and took her suitcases from the trunk of the car. Gripping the handle of one in each hand, she made her way back to the house. In the hall she set one down and carried the other with her as she mounted the stairs.

She wished either the housekeeper or the doctor was at home; she didn't like the idea of coming in and making herself right at home without their knowledge. She felt like a trespasser, even though in actual fact she had a legal right to be here.

Like downstairs, all the doors on the second floor were shut. Autumn tapped on the first one to her left and after a minute turned the knob and opened it. She could tell at a glance that it was used, for there were a few items on the dark black dresser across the room—probably the housekeeper's room. The room across the hallway was also used. A man's shirt was thrown carelessly across the bed and Autumn hastily closed that door again; it was obviously the doctor's bedroom. Further down the hall, on the left, was another bedroom which must have been used by Miss Hattie. There were photographs on the dresser and chest, a small bookcase next to the bed, and the mattress on the bed appeared to have been recently stripped, as though no longer needed.

The fourth room appeared to be unused. Although the fourposter bed was neatly made with a heavy white bedspread, there were no toiletries or other tell-tale personal possessions littering the dresser or chest of drawers.

Autumn set down her suitcase and looked around curiously at what would be her bedroom.

A minute later she went across the room to open a door to what she assumed was a clothes closet. But it was stuck. Using both hands to grasp the door handle, she tugged with all her might.

All at once the door flew open without warning and Autumn fell backwards. The door banged against the wall with a loud thud and she went tumbling across the foot of the bed.

When she had picked herself up and was rubbing her thigh tenderly, a voice, a vaguely familiar masculine voice said behind her, 'I knew you were coming some time soon, but did you have to make so much racket about it?'

Autumn whirled round. Behind her loomed the stranger who has changed her flat tire. Only now his skin and black hair glistened wetly. Gone were the baggy pants and, in their place, a neat pair of dark slacks that emphasised the lean, lithe legs they encased; gone was the plaid shirt and instead there was a broad expanse of bare chest with dark hair swirling in the centre very inadequately concealed by a yellow terry bath towel draped around his neck and a medallion hanging from a silver chain.

Autumn's eyes fixed on the medal, mesmerised. And for the life of her, she couldn't say a word.

CHAPTER TWO

HE stood there, towering over her, his Creole brown eyes raking her. 'It's customary to knock before you enter some-one else's home, even if you do happen to own it now,' he observed, as though he were teaching a backward child the social graces.

'I did knock,' Autumn said indignantly, recovering from her shock. 'At least, Ellis Naquin did, and he even came in with me and looked in all the downstairs rooms before he left. And when I came upstairs, I knocked before I looked in each bedroom. But you weren't anywhere. Where did you suddenly come from?' she demanded suspiciously.

'The shower,' he said briefly, rubbing a hand across his still wet hair. 'I'm sorry no one was available to greet the new owner of Bellefleur in the manner she doubtless ex-pected,' he added sarcastically, 'but I wasn't in the mood and Bertha is away.'

Autumn stared at him blankly, then she gasped breath-lessly, 'You're not ... you can't be ... you are Miss Hattie's nephew! The doctor!'

He gave a mock bow. 'I'm William Robichaux. Bill to my friends.' She wasn't sure if he was subtly telling her that she was not among them or if he was telling her she could call him that.

'But you took my five dollars this afternoon,' she said wonderingly as though it were the only important detail under discussion.

Unexpectedly, he laughed. Then his eyes levelled on her face again. 'Do you want it back?' he asked.

'Why did you take it?' she demanded irritably, not en-joying the joke at all. 'Why didn't you tell me who you were when you realised who I was?'

21

He was no longer laughing. His firm mouth drew into a straight, grim line. 'Miss Autumn McBride who didn't even do us the courtesy of letting us know she was coming? Miss Autumn McBride who was obviously so much above the lowly Cajun fisherman?' As she started to disclaim, he held up his hand to halt her. 'No,' he said in a hard voice, 'don't bother to deny it. It was easy enough to read your thoughts and opinion of me this afternoon. Why should I have bothered to tell you who I was? You wouldn't have believed me anyway.'

Autumn's gaze slid away from his face. He was perfectly right—she wouldn't have believed him. Besides which, at that time she had never heard of his existence, much less the fact that he had a right to share her new home.

'I'm right, aren't I?' His cold voice cut into her reflections.

Her head lifted proudly and sparks flashed in her eyes. 'If you are, it's only to be expected. You looked like a bum. What else was I supposed to think?'

'Just let that be a lesson to you that you can't always judge by appearances.' His eyes narrowed on her and then he added thoughtfully, 'Though sometimes it can be done. Take you, for instance. Dressed the way you are . . . looking the way you do . . . you're about as out of place here as a Louisiana alligator in the Nevada desert. Why don't you just turn around and go back where you belong, lady? You'll never fit in here.'

Autumn was so angry she was trembling. 'Whether I fit in here or not is my business, Doctor,' she all but spat at him. 'But I certainly won't turn tail and run at your displeasure!'

'Obviously there's no talking to you,' he said coldly, 'so I'll leave you.' He turned and walked out of the room. Autumn slammed the door furiously behind him, relieving some of the pent-up rage inside her. Oh, it was maddening! It was bad enough to find out that she had to share the house if she were to make her home here, but for it to be *him*, of all people! It would never work out, she was sure of that! She would have to see Mr Naquin again tomorrow and find out if there was some way to get around that section of the will. Because she was determined that if anyone were to leave this house, it would be Dr William Robichaux, not herself! She would *not* be packed off back to New York just because it might suit him better!

Half an hour later her temper had abated somewhat ... She set about unpacking the suitcase she had brought upstairs with her and when she was about to go back downstairs for the second one, she found it in the hallway, in front of her door. Dr Robichaux's temper must have cooled a bit, too.

Now that she thought about it, she couldn't really blame him for resenting her. Given the same circumstances, she knew she would resent an intruder, too. After all, he was Miss Hattie's nephew and it was natural to assume that as her only remaining relative, he would have inherited all of her estate. Instead, a total stranger, herself, had come in and been given his home. No, once she cooled down she could accept his anger and resentment. But, and now her chin stuck out determinedly, the fact remained that Bellefleur House *had* been willed to her and she intended to stay here in it, and no disgruntled relative was going to chase her away.

By the time she had put away all her clothes and washed up in the adjoining old-fashioned bathroom that she would obviously have to share with the doctor, since his shaving gear was strung all about in it, it was almost seven. Hunger pains assailed her. She had seen no sign of the housekeeper since she had been here, but she supposed that lady had surely returned home by now and had the dinner going. She decided to do downstairs and see.

When she entered the kitchen she drew up short in astonishment. With a white apron tucked into the waistband of his slacks, Dr Robichaux was busily tossing a salad.

As though he could feel her eyes on his back, he turned and saw her standing there. 'Hungry?' he asked as he turned back to the salad.

'Starving,' she admitted as she came further into the

room. 'But why are you preparing the meal? Where's the housekeeper?'

'I told you earlier ... she's away.'

'Away?' After a moment, sharply, 'Where's away?'

'Out of town away. Excuse me.' He reached past her and opened the cupboard to take out two individual salad bowls. While she watched, he expertly dished up the salad into the two bowls. 'Bertha has a sister who lives in Lafayette. The sister just had an operation, so Bertha's gone to stay with her until she's recovered. Understand?'

'But ... but that means we're alone here,' she stammered.

'Exactly.' His tone was easy. 'I see you do understand.'

'For the night?'

He turned suddenly to look at her, one hand on his hip. 'I might have known there'd be all this missishness, especially since this afternoon you kept expecting me to attack you instead of the flat tire.'

Autumn flushed and looked down at her hands. 'I ... I'm sorry,' she mumbled, 'but all the same I ...'

'I can promise you I don't have the least intention of laying a finger on you,' he told her dryly. 'You're not exactly on my favourite persons list, you know.'

Autumn's face turned even redder. 'I didn't say ... I didn't think ... oh, darn you, anyway! We can't stay here together all night because no matter what *doesn't* happen, people will believe it did.'

He yawned. 'What a naughty mind you have! Though I'm inclined to agree with you in this case. And it's *my* reputation I'm worried about, not yours! As the local doctor, I'm supposed to be an upholder of all the morals. However, since no one knows you're here with me alone, I suppose we can survive one night. Unless you want to drive all the way to Houma, that is, for a motel room.'

'How ... how far is that?' she asked nervously.

'About thirty miles.'

She was defeated and she knew it. She was tired and she was hungry, and it would be dark soon and it would be plain silly to allow herself to be driven out of her home to go in search of a motel room thirty miles away. Dr Robichaux read her decision in her face and nodded. 'Now you're being sensible. Reach into that cupboard on your left and you'll find the plates. You can set the table. Supper will be ready in five minutes.'

Autumn did as he bade her, relieved to be busy so that she wouldn't have to meet his eyes just yet. She was nervous enough about having to stay the night with him in the house, in spite of his reassurances, and she didn't want to read the jeering amusement in his eyes.

A few minutes later they were seated at the small kitchen table. He cut a huge piece of the steak he had grilled and placed it on her plate. With the salad and a baked potato, it made a delicious meal.

When they were halfway through, Autumn braved his possible sarcasm again by asking, 'When do you expect Mrs Guidry to return?'

'I'll telephone her after supper,' he said. 'We can get by tonight staying here alone, but it won't do for longer than that. The news will be getting around town that you're here. Tomorrow we'll definitely have to make some sort of different arrangements if Bertha can't make it back.' She nodded wordlessly and he went on, 'I'm afraid it's the best I can do at short notice.'

'I wasn't criticising,' she said humbly. 'And I realise that this situation is equally awkward for you. I'm just sorry I've caused so much trouble for you.'

His eyes were cool as they met hers. 'It could have been avoided entirely if you'd only let us know you were coming.'

She looked across at him and said earnestly, 'But I didn't know about you!'

'Didn't know?' She had clearly surprised him.

She shook her head. 'No. Mr Naquin sent me a letter explaining that I'd inherited a house from Miss Hattie. He never said it was a historic *plantation* house or that there were people living in it!'

'Is that true?' He looked at her quickly.

'Of course it's true!' she exclaimed indignantly. 'I'm not in the habit of lying.'

He shrugged. 'Then I guess that changes things. I'm angry enough over my aunt's will, of course, but that's hardly your fault. But I was angry that you had decided to come and move in without so much as a by-your-leave to me. I had no idea you'd be coming at all.'

Autumn grinned weakly. 'Big mix-up? And I thought you hated me because I was the recipient of the house!'

He got up and went to the stove and brought back the coffee pot. As he poured them each a cup, he said, 'Well, I'm not exactly thrilled about the business.'

'You mean—Aunt Hattie leaving the house to me?' Autumn asked as she spooned sugar into her cup. 'Mr Naquin said it must have been her way of showing gratitude for what I did when she was in New York.'

He sat down again and picked up his coffee. 'I guess. You saved her life there, she told me. I knew she was grateful, but not that she was that grateful.'

Autumn could not resist a retort. 'Meaning a life's not worth a house?'

He did not react. 'Meaning, I suppose, that I didn't realise her gratitude extended that far. After all, Bellefleur is our family home. My great-great-grandfather built it after he came here from France and made his fortune.'

Autumn looked down into the dark coffee before she took a sip of the strong chicory brew. 'I didn't know,' she said slowly. 'When I came, I expected an ordinary little house that a tiny spinster lady would own. I never dreamed it would be like this.' Suddenly angry, she demanded, 'What in the heck did come over her to do a thing like this? To both of us? And what are we going to do about it now?'

He shrugged. 'There's nothing we can do. The house is yours—that's all there is to it.'

Autumn looked at him shrewdly. 'Did you quarrel with her?'

He shook his head and ran long, bony fingers through his thick crop of hair. 'No,' he said, 'we never quarrelled. I adored her.' His voice was almost deliberately calm. 'She raised me from the time my parents died in a boating accident when I was five and she was just like a mother to me, right up to the day she died. It never entered my head that she would go and leave our home to a total stranger.'

'What about her mind?'

'Was it sound?' He laughed shortly. 'You met Aunt Hattie. Have *you* ever met anybody with a sounder head on their shoulders?'

Autumn laughed. 'No, I guess you're right. Even so, it's awfully strange.'

He scraped back his chair and stood up. 'Anyway, there's no use my crying over spilt milk. She left you the house and that's that. I guess I should be grateful that she included the instructions that I'm to be allowed to continue to live here. I would hate to have to suddenly move my practice.'

As he started to reach for a plate Autumn stood up, too. 'Please,' she said, 'let me do the dishes. After all, you cooked the meal.'

He swept his hand across the table in an expansive gesture. 'Be my guest,' he said easily. 'Did you get enough to eat? I'm afraid I haven't any dessert to offer you.'

'I couldn't eat another bite,' she said truthfully. 'But I am a bit surprised we didn't have fish for supper.'

'You mean the stringer of catfish I had this afternoon?' He grinned unexpectedly. 'Oh, I gave them away. Saved having to clean them that way.' Then he added, 'If you'll excuse me, I'll go to the library and call Bertha now.'

Autumn nodded absently and continued with her work. After he was gone, she wondered what to do. She was feeling worse by the minute because she was now the owner of Bellefleur when it was plain to anybody of the smallest intelligence that it should by rights have gone to Dr Robichaux. At the same time, the house was a thrilling sur-

prise to her and she hated to give it up at the outset. She had
come here prepared to live, but now, since it didn't seem
fair that she even had the house, she wondered if she
shouldn't just quietly go away again. Probably Mr Naquin
could draw up some legal paper for her that would sign the
ownership over to the doctor. All that would be fair to Bill
Robichaux, perhaps, but was it also fair to Autumn Mc-
Bride? It wasn't her fault that she hadn't known about any
nephew or that Miss Hattie hadn't left the house to him in
the first place. She had given up a very promising career to
come here and claim her inheritance. Was she now to be
denied it after all?

She was wiping the last dish when he returned. 'I got
through to Bertha and she agreed to return tomorrow night.
I'll pick her up at the bus station at nine,' he said.

'That's wonderful,' she responded as she hung the dish
towel on the rack.

'All finished here?' he asked. 'Let's sit in the library. It's
more comfortable than Aunt Hattie's parlour.'

A little later, as they were comfortably seated in deep
cushiony chairs, he asked suddenly, 'What did you do in
New York?'

'I was a model,' she answered simply.

His eyes studied her face keenly. 'It figures,' he said.
'And just what sort of modelling jobs do you expect to find
here in St Pierre?' There was a derisive sneer in his voice
and all her former dislike of him came swiftly back.

'I never expected to find any modelling jobs here at all,'
she said coldly.

'Did you plan to live off the fat of the land? If I remember
Aunt Hattie's will correctly, she left enough money to main-
tain the house with, but hardly enough to buy food and
clothing, too.'

'And I'm sure you've practically memorised that will by
now, haven't you?' she flared back. 'Where I get the money
to buy my food and clothes is no business of yours, Dr
Robichaux, but as a matter of fact, I expect to get a job to
support myself.'

He laughed abruptly. 'What sort of job? People around here have to *work* for a living, not just stand around looking beautiful. What do *you* know about work?'

Autumn glared at him. 'I was a secretary and a book-keeper before I became a model,' she informed him sharply. 'I expect I'll be able to find a job somewhere.'

He set his cup down on the table beside him, his gaze never once wavering from her face. 'Are you serious? You really are a secretary?'

She lifted her chin. 'I told you already that I'm not in the habit of lying. Why should I?'

He ignored that as he leaned forward towards her. 'I've got a job you can have, but it's temporary.'

'You?' She looked at him in surprise. 'What sort of job?' she asked warily.

'Secretary and receptionist. I had a nurse who also did the office work and answered the telephone, but she left a couple of months ago when she got married and moved away. Poor Bertha has tried to help me out ever since. She's been answering the telephone for me in the mornings, but it's not really her thing, and she doesn't know beans about secretarial work or bookkeeping. She'd be thrilled if you'd take it on.'

'You said it was temporary?'

He nodded. 'What I really need is another nurse who can do double duty—you know? Only nurses are hard to lure to small communities like this. But if you took this job, it would be with the understanding that I'm going ahead and looking for a nurse to take your place. But at least it would give you a job for the time being and help me out of a jam as well.'

Autumn thought about it for a moment. She was sure that Bill Robichaux would be the very devil to work for. As it was, it was bad enough that they were forced to share a house. But on the other hand, her financial resources were not without limits and there was the old saying about a bird in the hand and so forth. And there was no reason she couldn't be casting about for another job at the same time he was casting about for a nurse to take her place. With a sudden decisive nod, she agreed. 'All right, I'll take it.' And as she climbed the stairs a few minutes later she hoped she had made the right decision.

The following morning she was awakened by a knock on her door, followed by its opening. As her eyelids fluttered up, she saw Bill Robichaux poking his head round the door. 'Up and at 'em!' He followed his words in and deposited a tray on her bedside table. 'I brought you some *café au lait*.'

'Thanks,' she mumbled sleepily. Then, suddenly alert, she hastily pulled the covers up over her low cut black shorty pyjama top. Cautiously she propped herself up on her left elbow while her right hand maintained a firm grip on the concealing blanket at her throat. 'What time is it?'

'Six,' came the answer.

'A.M.?' she asked in amazement. 'Then why are you waking me?'

'You've got a job, remember? And the patients start coming at eight.'

'You'll get drummed out of the A.M.A. if you see patients before ten,' she told him scathingly. 'Besides, I never said I'd start working *today*! Go away. I'll start on Monday.' She laid her head back down on the pillow and closed her eyes.

The next instant she was sitting bolt upright. Dr Bill Robichaux had taken all her covers and thrown them to the foot of the bed, leaving her skimpily clad body fully exposed.

'How *dare* you!' she hissed at him murderously as she grabbed frantically for the blankets. 'Oh, you're just *too* much!'

She glared upwards at him, but he just stood there calmly surveying her, his arms crossed over his chest as though he had all day long to stand and watch a circus. She was only too aware what she looked like with her hair all over the place and her face still overlaid with sleep.

'Well,' he asked at last, 'are you going to get up or do I have to pick you up?'

She was just about to challenge him with the words, 'You wouldn't dare!' when she realised that he certainly would. So, after a moment's reflection, she twisted her body on the bed so that her feet touched the floor. Then her angry eyes met his again.

He nodded, as though satisfied, and moved to the door. 'Drink up your coffee,' he ordered. 'Breakfast in half an hour.'

As the door closed behind him, Autumn made a face in his general direction before she stood up. A moment later she was drinking the delicious coffee and having to admit to herself what a nice gesture *that* was anyway, before she went to take a shower.

Precisely thirty minutes later she entered the kitchen dressed in a bright yellow sleeveless summer dress. Her hair was swept up into a businesslike knot on top of her head.

Bacon, eggs and toast were on the table and Bill Robichaux was pouring fresh cups of coffee. 'Have a seat,' he told her, 'and eat up. This is the last meal I cook now that you're here.'

She didn't respond to that. She merely sat down and began to eat. A moment later she happened to look up and caught his eyes upon her. Startled and on the defensive, she challenged, 'Were you staring at me?'

'Was I?' He shook his head.

'Yes?'

'Well, you're not exactly going on a fashion parade. Couldn't you do something to deglamorise yourself before we go to the office?'

She stared at him as though he had lost his senses. 'Why?' she asked coldly.

He shrugged. 'It's just that my patients aren't used to a receptionist who looks as though she's stepped out of *Vogue*. I just don't want to start any talk.'

'I'm wearing one of the plainest, most businesslike

dresses I own,' she informed him frostily, 'and I can't get my hair into a more severe style than it's in now.'

'I suppose not,' he agreed as he studied her with a critical eye. 'The main problem is your face anyway. It's attractive.' The words were definitely not a compliment. Said like that, they were more of an accusation.

'You could get me a Hallowe'en mask,' she said sarcastically. He did not smile.

An hour later he ushered her through a connecting hallway, past a glass door that opened out on to an inviting courtyard and into his offices. He guided her into a room in the front which had an outside door. There was a receptionist's desk and numerous chairs and tables for waiting patients.

'Get ready for the onslaught,' he warned as he flipped open the appointment book. He indicated a filing cabinet. 'As each patient is shown in, bring their individual card to me from the file. And don't book appointments on Thursday or Saturday afternoons. Any questions we'll just have to deal with as we go along.'

Autumn nodded. Already there were several cars in the drive that came around to this side of the house. As he went to unlock the door, she asked, 'Are you the only doctor in town?'

He nodded. 'Yes. And believe me, they keep me running!' He headed towards the back where the examining rooms, X-ray room, lab and his private office were located. He turned slightly in the hallway and glanced back at her. 'Good luck,' he said unexpectedly.

Autumn smiled back. 'Thanks.'

They were the last private words they were to have all morning. The patients came in streams, all shapes and sizes and with every type of problem imaginable. Autumn was kept constantly busy. If she wasn't dealing with incoming patients, filling out forms, finding file cards or escorting patients to the examining rooms, she was answering the telephone and making future appointments or taking messages for the doctor to return calls later.

At noon she walked back to the lab with a message and Bill Robichaux looked at her closely. 'Tired?' he enquired.

'Maybe a little,' she admitted. 'Is it like this every day?'

He nodded. 'Just about, I'm afraid. How many patients are still out there?' he asked, jerking his thumb towards the waiting room.

'Three.'

He nodded. 'I'll see to them. You go and get some lunch.'

'What about you?' she asked as he turned back to his work.

'I'll get to it later,' he said vaguely. 'I've got a pretty heavy schedule today.'

Autumn left and went out through the connecting door into the main part of the house. She found some left-over ham in the refrigerator, so she busied herself making sandwiches.

Twenty minutes later she was back in the office. Four new patients had arrived. She went straight to the back and again found the doctor in the lab. 'I've made you some ham sandwiches,' she told him quietly. 'They're on the kitchen table. Go and eat them.'

'How many patients are waiting to see me?' he asked.

'Four. There'll soon be more, but they can wait. You haven't stopped for an instant all morning. You must go and eat.'

He looked at her as though in surprise at being ordered around. Then, 'All right,' he agreed, 'I'll go. Hold the fort down, I'll be back in fifteen minutes.' As she turned to leave he said quietly from behind her, 'Autumn?'

She turned to face him and he smiled. 'Thanks.'

'For what?'

'The sandwiches. What else?' Then he was gone.

The afternoon was as busy as the morning. By five-thirty Autumn was feeling quite frazzled. And there were still a few patients waiting to see the doctor.

The telephone rang and she dealt with it. When she hung up, she was suddenly aware that someone was behind her. It was Bill Robichaux. 'Time for you to knock off for the day,' he said in a low voice that couldn't carry across the room to the waiting patients.

'Yes, but you've still got people to see you.'

'I know, but you can leave anyway. I'll deal with them.'

She met his eyes seriously. 'Are you sure? I don't mind staying.'

He grinned suddenly. 'I'd rather you'd go fix us some supper,' he admitted. 'Those sandwiches didn't stick.'

Autumn smiled in sympathy. 'Mine either,' she acknowledged. 'All right, if you're sure then, I'll go get something started.' She rose and went through the connecting door into the house.

As she went down the hall on the other side of the connecting door, she was mentally wondering what she could possibly prepare for their meal. At noon she had been in such a hurry she hadn't thought about taking any meat from the freezer so it could thaw in time for supper. Now she was wondering if there was a food market close by.

She reached the main hallway and turned towards the kitchen. And in that instant a delicious aroma wafted towards her.

She entered the kitchen to find a plump lady standing in front of the stove. She had wiry salt-and-pepper hair and a big smile of welcome.

'You must be Mrs Guidry!' Autumn exclaimed.

'Call me Bertha,' the lady told her. 'And you are the new owner of Bellefleur,' she stated. 'Autumn no?'

'Yes.' Autumn held out a hand and as they shook hands she added, 'Dr Robichaux said you wouldn't be back until late tonight. In fact, he mentioned having to pick you up at the bus station.'

Bertha shrugged dismissively. 'I got a ride back from Lafayette. A friend who lives over in Thibodeaux was coming back himself.'

'How nice,' said Autumn. 'And how is your sister?'

'She's doing pretty good now. It was no problem to leave her, no. I'm happy to be back home.'

'I'm glad. I hate to be such trouble to everybody.'

'You're no trouble, *chère*,' said Bertha, smiling. 'Miss Hattie, she wanted you to have this house, so I'm glad you're here, yes. Now, how soon you and Dr Billy want to eat?'

'I'm not sure. He still had a few patients waiting to see him. I came back so I could start supper, but instead I find a delicious smell. What is that you're cooking, Bertha?'

'Shrimp gumbo.' She eyed Autumn's slender figure critically. 'You like gumbo?'

'I don't know,' Autumn admitted truthfully. 'I've never eaten it. But if it tastes anywhere near as good as it smells, I'm bound to love it. And am I starving!'

'Hmph,' Bertha sniffed disapprovingly. 'You're so skinny, looks to me like you don't eat enough to keep a humming bird alive, you. Are you a picky eater? Or is it you don't know how to cook for yourself up there in New York?'

Before she could frame an answer, one came from behind her. 'Autumn is a model, Bertha,' Bill Robichaux said over her shoulder. 'All models have to know how to do is to look pretty at all times.'

CHAPTER THREE

AUTUMN whirled, high colour stinging her cheeks. 'It seems to me that I accomplished a bit more than just looking pretty today in the office!'

She saw a mocking look in his eyes as he gazed down at her face from his superior height. 'I must agree,' he said. 'You've certainly started out like a house afire, but it remains to be seen just how long you'll keep it up. But I give you fair warning now, the first time I find you polishing your fingernails on the job, you're fired.' While Autumn was still attempting to think up a fitting retort, he added to the housekeeper, 'Glad you're back, Bertha. Give me fifteen minutes to bath and change before dinner, will you?' With that, he vanished through the door as Autumn glared after him.

Her eyes glittered. 'He has a nerve!' she muttered through gritted teeth. 'I worked really hard today and he knows it!'

Bertha smiled calmly as she lifted the heavy black lid from the pot on the stove and thrust a spoon down into the dark, hot liquid. 'Still, he's warning you true, *chère*. Dr Billy, he expects a woman to be useful, not just decorative.'

'And can't a girl be both?' Autumn demanded.

Bertha shrugged her shoulders. 'Not in Dr Billy's books. He has no use for the pretty fripperies of life. I guess he's worked too hard all his life.'

Autumn placed both hands on her hips. 'But it's unfair for him to take such an attitude towards me!'

Bertha smiled. 'Maybe so,' she agreed, 'but he has his reasons for feeling that way, yes. When he was just a poor struggling intern, he was engaged to a beautiful local girl, but she threw him over for a rich man who was old enough

36

to be her father. Since then, Dr Billy hasn't had much use for beautiful girls, no. Except,' she added musingly, 'that lately he's been seeing quite a bit of his old love now that she's a widow.' She gave an expressive shrug. 'Some time men don't ever learn, now, do they?' Then she added to a still fuming Autumn, 'You'll just have to prove to him that you're both beautiful and useful, no, *chère*?'

'I will,' Autumn vowed. 'And I'll make him eat his words!'

Bertha laughed at her earnestness and waved a shooing hand at her. 'In the meantime, get out of my kitchen and let me finish up with supper. Me, I cook best when I'm not being interrupted, yes.'

Autumn took her dismissal in good graces, but the doctor's words still rankled a while later when the two of them sat together at the big dining room table. She was dismayed to learn from Bertha that she preferred to take her meals alone either in the kitchen or on a tray in the old-fashioned parlour. That meant that Autumn herself was stuck with Bill alone at meals, and just now she was too angry with him even to attempt polite conversation after his implication that she hadn't pulled her weight today.

Even worse, he didn't seem to take her anger seriously. A couple of times he attempted to engage her in conversation, but each time she cut him dead, and thereafter once or twice she thought she detected a look of amusement on his face, which only served to increase her annoyance.

When they were finished with the meal at last and Autumn would have gone upstairs, he forestalled her by laying a detaining hand on her arm. 'Shall we walk down to the bayou while it's still light?'

She wanted to refuse him haughtily, but the truth was she badly needed some fresh air after being cooped inside all day long. Also, there was a jut to his chin that gave her the impression that he would refuse to accept 'no' for an answer. So with a deep sigh, she nodded. 'All right,' she agreed.

'Your enthusiasm overwhelms me,' he said dryly.

She gave him a withering glance before she swept out of
the room and down the wide central hall.

Outside, away from the coolness of the air-conditioned
rooms, the air was hot and humid. There had been a rain
shower during the early afternoon, but rather than cool
things off, it had only made things more stifling.

They walked silently down a path lined with azalea
bushes. Autumn's back was ramrod straight. She wished
Bill wouldn't walk so close behind her—she could feel
prickles on her neck.

'Did you see anything of New Orleans on your way
down?' he enquired conversationally.

'The traffic,' she answered snappishly. From the corner of
her eye she could see his lips twitch, and she longed to be
able to hit him. Never in all her life had she had such feelings of antagonism towards anyone so often as she had
with this man in the short time since they had met.

The silence stretched out between them for a time until
at last he said, 'Would it please you if I apologised?' His
tone was the reverse of apologetic.

'Why do you have it in for me?' she demanded crossly.
'Why do you think that just because my face is ... is ...'

'Is beautiful,' he supplied easily.

'Why should that mean I would shirk work?' she went on
doggedly.

He shrugged. 'It's just my opinion that a beautiful woman
such as yourself would find it beneath her. However, you
did an excellent job today and as long as you keep it up,
there's no problem, is there? So let's drop the subject,' he
added in a bored voice. 'Tell me, how do you like Bertha?'

She was about to give another clipped reply, but her
mouth curved involuntarily. 'I like her a lot,' she admitted.
'And I like the way she talks—her accent.'

'Her Cajun dialect?'

'Is that what it is? I've never heard it before. It has a
really quaint sound.'

He nodded. 'You'll be hearing a lot of it in this section

of Louisiana. It's a patois mixture of a little bit of everything, but it derives chiefly from the archaic form of French
that the Acadians spoke in Nova Scotia and that the people
brought with them when they were dispersed from there.'

'Oh, I know!' she exclaimed as light dawned. 'Longfellow's poem, *Evangeline*.'

'Right.'

Autumn shook her head. 'My history is pretty bad,
though. Tell me about them. Why were they sent away
from their homes?'

'Acadia was a French settlement, but after the Queen
Anne War in 1713 it became an English holding. Only the
Acadians' sympathies were with the French and they caused
a lot of trouble for the British. In 1755, the British tried to
force them to take an oath of allegiance to the English king.
Those who refused were deported, and some of those who
were exiled ended up in south Louisiana and have since
become known as Cajuns.'

'And *Evangeline* was about that wandering for a place to
settle, wasn't it? And lovers becoming separated?'

'Yes. There's a legend about the real Evangeline, whom
Longfellow fashioned his heroine after. Her name was
Emmeline Labiche. She became separated from her fiancé,
Louis Arceneaux, the Gabriel of the poem, and eventually
trailed him to a landing place of the Acadians called Poste
des Attakapas on Bayou Teche. Only, unlike the poem, he
was faithless and, when she found him, he was betrothed
to another. They say she lost her mind over it. She died
a short time later and you can see her grave still, in the
Poste des Attakapas cemetery. In St Martinville there's a
tree beneath which they say Emmeline met Louis when she
arrived. Maybe one day we can drive over there for you to
see it, hmm?'

'No, thanks,' she said, shaking her head. 'I have no desire
to see the spot where a faithless lover's cruel words crushed
a poor girl to the point of driving her mad and to her death.'
A certain bitterness had crept into her voice as she thought

about Don and his threat, probably fulfilled by now, of
bringing another girl to live with him if she wouldn't. She
had been crushed, too, but she was made of sterner stuff
than the tragic Emmeline. Never would she love a man so
much that to lose him meant the end of her life.

'Ah,' he drawled. 'You condemn poor Louis for his un-
faithfulness, yet he truly believed he would never see
Emmeline again. Could your love for a man be as strong as
Evangeline's, which took her searching for her Gabriel
for years and was still with her when they finally met again
as he was an old and dying man?'

They had come to a halt on the banks of the bayou that
threaded its way between the spreading oaks. Bullfrogs
croaked and katydids lifted their shrill music in honour of
the coming night. Autumn shrugged her shoulders delicately as she stood gazing at the murky waters. 'I don't
know,' she admitted at last. 'But that was fiction, after all.
Emmeline was real and she must have loved Louis very
much to follow him all the way from Novia Scotia to Louisiana. It's a shame,' she added dryly, 'that his love wasn't as
strong as hers. If it had been, he would have searched for
her as well.'

'And if he never found her? Was he to be condemned to
a lifetime of loneliness?' His voice was compelling and low
as he stood beside her.

She was silent for a long time. 'Perhaps not,' she acknowledged at last.

'You know,' he continued in the same low, even voice,
'you have an air of a person who's running away from
someone rather than to him. The man you left behind ...
do you expect him to follow after you the way Evangeline
did Gabriel?'

'No!' she exclaimed sharply. And then she realised she
had given away a lot with the one word. She glared at him
angrily. 'Stop probing,' she ordered. 'My private concerns
are just that ... private.'

He shrugged his shoulders. 'I tried to stay out of your

private concerns yesterday,' he told her. 'But you asked me to change your tire.'

Autumn's lips curled derisively. 'Do you get nosy about the personal affairs of every girl whose flat tire you've changed?'

He laughed outright and, unexpectedly, reached out and brushed a tendril of copper-toned hair away from her face where a sudden puff of breeze had blown it. 'No, my dear,' he said. 'Only those girls who move into my home and office. And now perhaps we'd better go back inside. I see Bertha waving at us—some emergency must have cropped up.'

He was right. Bertha gave him the message that somebody's child had cut itself badly. Bill grabbed up his black bag and headed outside again, this time towards the garage. Autumn watched him drive away in his cream-coloured L.T.D. 'Yesterday,' she said to Bertha behind her, 'he was driving a horrible old black truck.'

Bertha laughed. 'Oh, that'd be Smitty's truck down at the garage. If he was servicing Dr Billy's car, then he probably lent him the truck until he was finished.'

Autumn grimaced to herself. That truck, as much as the careless way Bill had been dressed, had made her think him unsavoury. And he had enjoyed her misconceptions wholeheartedly.

That night, in her bedroom, Autumn filed her nails. Not only would she never dream of polishing them on the job as Bill had taunted, but she wouldn't file them there either. And filed they had to be. Long fingernails just didn't go with typewriters, she thought with a sigh of regret. She had been rather proud of her long, tapered nails and she hated to see them pared down to a utilitarian length. However, what must be done must be done. She smiled grimly to herself as she thought about what her old room-mate, Joyce, would say if she could only see her now, filing her nails and hunting out plain, serviceable dresses for work in a small town doctor's office.

The next morning Autumn found herself quite busy again at the office. The waiting room was filled to overflowing, as though the citizens of St Pierre, knowing their one and only doctor would be off in the afternoon and all of Sunday, were trying to get all of their medical affairs in order before he got away.

One harassed-looking young mother brought in her five small children who were suffering with bronchial infections and colds. She looked so whipped down by the enormity of five ill children at once that Autumn couldn't help but feel sorry for her. Even so, that didn't explain why, when after they had left, Bill came to her desk and told her quietly, 'Don't send a bill to Mrs Broussard.'

She lifted quizzical eyebrows. 'Don't?'

'Don't,' he repeated curtly, with a forbidding expression, before he turned away and went back into his own office.

At noon, like the day before, Bill dismissed her even though there were still a couple of patients waiting to see him. Autumn went through the connecting hallway back to the main part of the house and found Bertha preparing their lunch.

'There seemed to be a lot of cars coming and going today,' she greeted Autumn. 'Dr Billy must be very busy, no?'

'Yes, it has been busy. He's still got a couple of patients to see, but he should be through soon.'

Bertha nodded. 'When I went outside to take John, the gardener, a cold drink, I thought I saw Lettie Broussard. Are some of her children sick?'

'The lady with the five small stair-steps?' Autumn asked. As Bertha nodded, she said, 'Yes. All of them.'

Bertha clicked her tongue in sympathy. 'The poor thing! Only four months ago her husband died. He was bad sick for the past year and in and out of hospital—cancer, you know, nothing they could do for him. He didn't leave no insurance either. It's a downright shame, yes.'

So that was the explanation of Bill's mysterious order not to bill Mrs Broussard. He was softhearted about some things, anyway, only he hadn't wanted her to guess.

That afternoon Bertha took Autumn on a tour to the one part of the house she had not yet had time to explore—the twin to Bill's offices—the right wing.

As Bertha unlocked the connecting door, she explained, 'Miss Hattie's old brother, George, lived here for the last ten years of his life. He was an old bachelor who loved his drink just a bit too much,' she said with a twinkle in her eyes. 'Miss Hattie, she didn't approve, and they got into some fierce arguments about it.' She chuckled, as if remembering some quite amusing scene. 'So the upshot was that he moved into this wing and they only saw each other after that by appointment.'

As Autumn entered what was obviously a living room, she could see a kitchen behind it. 'Why, it's a complete, separate apartment, isn't it?' she exclaimed in surprise.

'Yes,' Bertha agreed. 'Like I said, Mr George and Miss Hattie, they lived separate lives here.'

Autumn toured the entire apartment silently, taking in everything. Old George must have been something. It was quite apparent that old-fashioned he had definitey not been. The living room boasted a plush gold tweed-covered sofa and chair with modern coffee and lamp tables. The bedrooms, two of them, also had modern furniture, and the kitchen and bath were as up-to-date as any woman could wish, in vivid yellows and greens.

They went back along the hall and into the main part of the house once again. 'How long ago did Mr George die?' she asked.

Bertha squinted as her face took on a thoughtful expression. 'Let me see now. It was two year ago last April.'

'And the apartment has been closed up ever since?'

The older woman nodded.

'Well, you know,' Autumn ventured as she watched Bertha turn to lock the connecting door behind them, 'it's a wonderful little apartment. It's a shame for it to go to waste like that. I bet we could rent it out.'

'Are you serious about that?' a familiar voice interrupted.

Autumn hadn't been aware that Bill was even still in the house, much less behind her. She turned to see that he had replaced the shirt, tie and white jacket of the office for a casual white knit pullover top with cream-coloured slacks. The lightness of the clothes emphasised his dark good looks.

'Serious about what?' she asked. 'Renting the apartment?' At his nod, she said lightly, 'Why not? Know of anyone suitable?'

To her surprise, he nodded. 'I might. I was talking to Ed Weber, the principal of the high school, the other day and he happened to mention that one of his new teachers is looking for a place to live when school starts. Apartments are kind of hard to come by in St Pierre, so he's probably still looking.'

'Single? Married? Children?' Autumn asked.

Bill frowned in quick concentration. 'I believe Ed said he was married, but I'm not sure about children. Why don't I call him and see?'

She nodded. 'Would you?'

She went with him to the library while he made the call and when he hung up, he said, 'It's a young married couple, and as of yesterday they still didn't have a place to live. Right now they're still in New Orleans, their home, and Ed gave me their telephone number. I'm going to New Orleans this afternoon anyway, so I'll call them for you if you like. That way, maybe they could drive over tomorrow to look at the apartment. School will be starting here in another week.'

'That's fine,' Autumn agreed. 'Bertha and I will give it a good airing this afternoon. It seemed kind of musty from being closed up for so long.'

A few minutes later Bill left and Autumn went to the kitchen to ask Bertha's help in airing the apartment. 'It's really clean,' Autumn noted. 'Only a little dusty.'

Bertha obligingly gathered dusting cloths, polish and the vacuum cleaner. 'We'll soon have it spick and span, us, working together.'

As Bertha once again unlocked the connecting door to the

right wing, the telephone rang in the library. Autumn grimaced and handed her gear over to Bertha. 'I'll get it. It's probably someone trying to reach the doctor.'

But instead it was Ellis Naquin, sounding cheerful and carefree. 'I was wondering if you'd have dinner with me tonight at the Country Club.'

'I'd love it,' Autumn responded at once. She had done nothing but work the two days she had been here and had seen nothing of St Pierre, much less its more pleasant attractions. She felt she had well earned an outing, so Ellis's invitation came at a time that made it most appealing.

'Good,' he answered. 'There'll be dancing, too. I'll pick you up at seven.'

For the remainder of the afternoon Autumn and Bertha worked on the apartment, Autumn polishing furniture, Bertha vacuuming floors and window blinds. Windows were thrown open so that fresh air could blow away some of the musty smell.

When they were finished, Bertha stood surveying their work, hands on hips, and said, 'It'll be good to have someone living here again, yes. Miss Hattie didn't see much of her brother, but Dr Billy used to stop in to visit with him every evening and sometimes if he had to leave early Mr George would make me come and play checkers with him.' She laughed. 'How he loved those checkers! I kind of miss those times. But if we get some new people in here, it won't seem like such a lonely place any more, no.'

They returned to the main section of the house and stored away their cleaning supplies in the pantry. 'I suppose you miss Miss Hattie too, don't you?' Autumn ventured.

Bertha sighed. 'I sure do. I was with her for twenty-five year, since right after my husband died. We didn't have no children, so I was happy coming to help take care of a little boy—took away the loneliness. And Miss Hattie and me, we grew to be close-close, almost like sisters, yes.'

'Twenty-five years!' exclaimed Autumn. 'I would think

so. And I'll bet you had a hard time coping with Bill as a child!'

Bertha chuckled indulgently. 'Oh, he was a card, that one! There wasn't nothing he wouldn't try, no! See these grey hairs?'

Autumn laughed with her. 'Some day when we've got time,' she said, 'you'll have to tell me about them.' She could just imagine that Bill Robichaux must have been a real terror when he was young.

That evening Autumn surveyed herself critically in the mirror of the old-fashioned dresser in her bedroom. She was wearing a floor-length gold dress that lent golden highlights to her coppery hair. 'You'll do,' she told herself laughingly before turning away from the mirror. She refused to dwell upon the fact that it was a dress that Don had been particularly fond of. The thought of him was still too raw, too painful. That was why she had been glad that the past couple of days had been so exceedingly busy ... it gave her less time to think of what she had lost back in New York.

And yet, she told herself as she descended the curving staircase, if she were back there now and had it all to go through again, knowing as she did now that he would let her go, she would still do the same. Though she still loved him, even now she would not allow it to alter her decision not to move in with him. A lot of girls did it these days, of course, and it didn't seem to bother them at all. But though she felt they had a perfect right to live their lives the way they wanted, without criticism, she would never be among their number. For all that she looked and dressed modern and up-to-date, the truth was she was old-fashioned. She wanted the traditional scene of marriage, home and a family, permanent fixtures for her life.

The front door bell rang and she was glad of the distraction. She thrust the memory of Don into the deepest recesses of her mind and went across the wide hallway to open the door.

An hour later Ellis Naquin was asking, 'Sure you wouldn't like a dessert?'

Autumn groaned in mock dismay as the white-coated waiter placed a rich dessert before Ellis. 'I couldn't possibly eat another bite! As it is, I'm terrified that I'm going to put on too much weight here, anyway.'

'Anyone as slender as you can afford an extra pound or two,' he told her.

'That's just what a model can't do,' she told him. 'A pound or two now becomes three or four before you realise it.'

'Ah, but you're no longer a model, are you? You gave it up when you came here, didn't you?'

'True,' she admitted with a smile. 'But you never know ... I may get tired of St Pierre and head back to the bright lights.'

'Then we'll just have to see to it that we keep you entertained here, won't we?' At her laugh, he went on, 'I hear through the town grapevine that you've become the doctor's new receptionist.'

'That's right,' she agreed. 'Temporarily, anyway.'

'How did Robichaux accept the fact of your moving in?' he asked curiously as he spooned up some of his chocolate.

'Not too well at first,' she acknowledged. 'But I guess you could say we've reached a truce for now.' Her lips curved slightly as she recalled that explosive meeting in her bedroom. The picture of Bill striding purposely into her room, bare-chested, the shock of him being the same man who'd changed her tire, were all things that were indelibly printed in her mind.

She and Ellis ate leisurely and sat chatting quietly over the coffee afterwards. When they had first arrived there had been few other diners like themselves, but during the time they had been here quite a few new patrons had arrived, so that now there was a large gathering as the band on the raised dais across the room began playing their first number.

'Would you like to dance?' Ellis asked. His light brown

eyes regarded her admiringly. 'I must show you off.'

'Show me off?' she said with a slight feeling of irritability.
'You make me sound like the first prize trophy at the school
bike rodeo!'

His arm tightened around her as they began to dance.
'Much, much nicer a trophy than that,' he told her. 'And I
must let everyone see that the trophy *is* mine.'

Autumn drew away from him stiffly, forcing his arm
round her to slacken a little. 'I'm nobody's trophy or prize,'
she told him firmly. 'I belong to myself.'

Unabashed, Ellis grinned at her as he tightened his hold
on her waist once again. 'Don't look so stern, my dear. You
can't blame a guy for trying, you know. 'Oh, damn,' he
added in a different voice. 'It seems I'm going to have to
share you with others already—some friends of mine are
waving insistently. Shall we go and join them?'

The three people at the table next to the dance floor regarded Autumn with frank curiosity. Ellis introduced her.
'Autumn, I'd like you to meet St Pierre's mayor, Lester
LeCompte, and his wife Bonnie.' Autumn shook hands with
the friendly-looking man and his smiling wife. They appeared to be in their middle thirties.

'Excuse our rude stares,' Mrs LeCompte told her. 'It's
only that unknown beautiful young women hardly ever visit
our little community, so we couldn't help but be curious.'

Now Ellis was introducing her to the remaining woman
who sat at the table. 'This is Pauline Blanchard,' he told her.

Autumn looked into ice-blue eyes and felt slightly chilled
by the encounter. The woman was daintily beautiful ...
petite, with raven black curls nestled against her face and a
creamy magnolia complexion, the sort of woman whom men
knocked themselves out to wait upon in every way possible.
But here was no friend to other women, Autumn instinctively knew, and herself in particular. Antagonism flowed
without a word ever having been spoken.

Autumn felt disconcerted to have such negative vibra-
tions about a total stranger and she could only hope, as she

and Pauline Blanchard went through the formal motions of introduction, that no one else could detect their instant and mutual dislike.

'She's no visitor,' Ellis informed the others as the two of them sat down at the table. 'Autumn has moved here for good. She's inherited Bellefleur from Hattie Robichaux.'

'Why, that's wonderful!' Lester LeCompte said heartily. 'We hope you'll be happy here.'

'I'm sure I shall, Mayor,' Autumn responded with a smile. 'St Pierre seems to be a very pretty town.'

He beamed at her. 'We're proud of it,' he told her. 'But don't call me Mayor ... that way's too formal. My name's Les and I'm close friends with Bill Robichaux, whom I suppose you've already met, seeing you're the new owner of Bellefleur.'

'Are you actually *living* at Bellefleur?' Pauline Blanchard asked sharply.

'Yes, I am.'

'With Bill?' The inflection in her voice left no doubt of her meaning.

'Bertha Guidry lives there, too,' Autumn said evenly.

'But if you're the new owner, won't Bill be moving out?' the dark-haired girl demanded insistently.

'Not unless he chooses to do so,' Autumn answered. 'The will says he's to have a home and his office at Bellefleur for as long as he wishes. Isn't that right, Ellis?' she asked, turning to her lawyer escort.

He nodded to the others who were all listening interestedly. 'Yes. Of course, I'm sure Robichaux will be making some kind of plans for moving in the future. After all, he's a reasonable man and it stands to reason that the man Autumn marries won't care to have a doctor's office right there in the house. That's if Autumn continues to live at Bellefleur after her marriage.'

Now Pauline smiled graciously at her. 'Oh, are you going to be married soon?' Her voice was syrupy sweet and Autumn suddenly felt slightly nauseous.

'No,' she answered just as sweetly. 'I don't plan to marry for years and years yet.' She had the satisfaction of seeing Pauline Blanchard's obvious expression of dismay.

'Well,' Ellis piped up, 'you never know what the future holds.'

'That's the truth,' Bonnie LeCompte agreed. 'Why, Les and I grew up next door to each other, yet it never entered my head I'd want to marry him until he came home one Christmas holiday from college.'

'Yeah,' Lester laughed teasingly. 'And then I was so irresistible that she married me that very summer.'

'Yes,' Bonnie said equably, 'but what he's not telling you is that I gave up a chance to study in Paris for a year by marrying *him*!'

Everyone laughed at their good-natured banter, and then Pauline fixed her attention back upon Autumn. 'By the way,' she said, almost too casually, 'where is Bill? I half expected to see him here tonight. He often comes here for dinner on the weekends. Is he out making house calls instead of insisting that his patients see him only during regularly scheduled office hours?'

Autumn assumed Bill had driven to New Orleans this afternoon to keep a date with a girl-friend there, because he had certainly looked anything but businesslike when he'd left and he hadn't offered any explanation of where he was going. But she wasn't going to go into speculation about this with Pauline. Now she shrugged her shoulders delicately. 'I'm afraid I don't have the least idea where he is this evening,' she said casually, 'but I'd be happy to give him a message for you if you like.'

Pauline looked slightly taken aback. 'A message?'

Autumn nodded and struggled to hold back a smile. 'Yes. I'm his new office receptionist, you see. It's part of my job to take messages for him. I assure you I won't forget to give it to him.'

Pauline gave her a dagger-sharp look. 'No message, thank you,' she said. 'What Bill and I have to say to each other is quite private. It couldn't be entrusted to a third party, I'm afraid.'

Was the other girl subtly warning her off Bill Robichaux? Autumn wondered with amusement. She had her answer a few minutes later when, back at their own table, Ellis said, 'Pauline is a widow. Her husband, who was much older than her, died two years ago. He had some oil interests and I understand he left her quite well off financially. Town gossip is that she wants our local doctor as hubby number two.'

'And is he likely to oblige her?' Autumn asked. Somehow the thought of Bill married to Pauline Blanchard bothered her, but she could not think why.

Ellis shrugged. 'Can't tell. Nobody ever knows exactly how Robichaux feels about any woman. But he does seem to see Pauline quite often, and they were engaged back when he was a struggling intern. But instead she married Blanchard. So what will happen this time around is anybody's guess.'

Well, one thing was for sure, Autumn thought. If Bill was going to marry Pauline, then he had a nerve criticising Autumn herself about being merely pretty and unuseful to society. If she ever saw a female who appeared to be an utter stranger to work, it was Pauline Blanchard. She would have thought Bill would choose someone quite different from a girl who would marry a man much older than herself because he had a lot of money. Because she was as sure as she was sitting here that Pauline had not married for such a simple reason as love. What woman in her right mind would marry an older man when she might have a man like Bill Robichaux, unless it was for the money?

She jerked her thoughts back to the present, deliberately dismissing both Pauline Blanchard and Bill Robichaux from her thoughts. She had come here to have fun this evening, not to waste time thinking about the man who happened to share her home.

CHAPTER FOUR

IT was late when Ellis drove his car across the bridge over the bayou, which he told Autumn was named Bayou Cache. The summer night was so inky black that Autumn couldn't see the water. Its darkness merged with the banks and the overhanging trees.

The car drew to a stop in the circular driveway and Ellis came around to open Autumn's door. As they walked up the steps of the house, she began, 'I really had a wonderful evening, Ellis.'

They stopped before the door and his hands captured hers. He drew her towards him. 'I've had a wonderful time, too,' he told her huskily, and bent his head, about to kiss her, to her dismay.

She drew back sharply, whispering, 'Oh, no, no!' when suddenly the porch light flashed on, momentarily blinding them.

The front door opened, spilling out more light from the hallway, and framed in the opening was Bill Robichaux. 'Oh, sorry,' she heard him say. 'I heard a noise and thought it might be someone coming to talk to me. I didn't mean to intrude.' There was a sarcastic note to his voice that infuriated Autumn.

By now she had freed her hands from Ellis's. Embarrassed at the situation, she snapped angrily at Bill, 'You didn't intrude on a thing. We were merely saying goodnight.' She turned to face Ellis again and forced a smile. 'Goodnight, and thank you again for such a pleasant evening,' she told him.

His face was a picture of thwarted desire. 'Goodnight,' he said in a defeated voice. 'I'll call you tomorrow.' With a curt nod at Bill he turned and ran down the steps.

Bill backed away from the doorway just a little, giving Autumn room to squeeze past him and into the hall. She was self-consciously aware of his eyes on her back as she went towards the staircase.

'I'm sorry if I embarrassed you,' he said without any sound of apology in his voice, 'but I had no idea you were even out. I just got home from New Orleans a little while ago and I assumed you were in bed asleep.'

'You did *not* interrupt anything,' she said coldly. She wasn't about to tell him that despite her embarrassment she was really rather glad he had opened that door when he did, that he came at just the right time to freeze Ellis's ardour. 'I was only saying goodnight,' she repeated.

He came towards her until he was standing directly in front of her, only a foot away. Once again she was aware of his immense height and how she felt dwarfed by it. With her high heels on she had been the same height as Ellis, which was quite usual with the men she dated. But next to Bill Robichaux she felt small, and it was an odd sensation to have to lift her face to meet his eyes.

'I hope,' he said slowly, 'you aren't going to make a habit of staying out late on week nights, too. I'm a very light sleeper and I would hate to be awakened unless someone was ill and needed me.'

'Don't let it worry you,' she said frostily. 'I'll be as quiet as a mouse whenever I come in late.' With that she turned and swept up the stairs, with her spine tingling beneath his gaze.

In the morning she was awakened by a thundering knock on her door. Before she could rouse herself, the door opened and Bill was there, a tray in his hand. 'Rise and shine,' she heard him say. 'I've brought your coffee.'

'What time is it?' she asked drowsily as she automatically pulled the covers up to her chin.

'Six-thirty.'

'On a Sunday morning?' She demanded with sheer incredulity, her eyes wide open now. 'You must be crazy!

I like to sleep in late on Sundays.'

'And miss the best part of the day,' he observed. As she sat up he took her pillows and propped them up behind her head. When she leaned back against them he handed her the cup of coffee, then sat down on the edge of the bed as though there was nothing odd about it at all and as though he had all the time in the world to sit and chat. 'I thought you'd like to come to eight o'clock Mass with me. Bertha likes to get her Sunday dinner cooked before she goes to the eleven o'clock service. Well, what do you say, *chère*? Eight or eleven?'

'Oh, now I'm awake, I'll make the eight o'clock,' she told him, aware that she was falling in with his wishes.

They walked to St Joseph's. The church was only three blocks away once they were across the bayou. Autumn had to admit to herself that Bill had something about this being the best part of the day. Although the sun was bright and the air still, the day was not yet hot as it would be later.

After Mass, he introduced her to a large number of other churchgoers, whose names she promptly forgot since there were so many of them. Apparently most of St Pierre had already learned who she was and that she was now the owner of Bellefleur, because though each person welcomed her with a friendly word and a smile, no one seemed surprised at her being among them.

At noon Bertha served fried chicken with the inevitable rice and gravy. Afterwards, Autumn insisted upon cleaning the kitchen herself while Bertha went upstairs to take a well-deserved Sunday afternoon nap.

To her surprise, Bill came to help her by drying the dishes. 'You don't have to do that,' she told him.

'No?' He smiled. 'But then neither do you. Strictly speaking, it's Bertha's job. So I suppose if you can help her out, I can help you out. Okay?'

She laughed a little. 'Okay.' Bill was such a mystery to her. He could be rude and nasty, haughty and off-putting, helpful and kind, friendly and fun. She'd never met a man before who was so consistently inconsistent. At times when he brought her coffee in bed, or called her *chère*, or, like now, was helpful and nice, it was easy to warm up to him and believe they could be friends. But at times when he scorned her ability to be a real and useful member of society just because of her looks, or, like last night, was rude and sarcastic, she was sure they wouldn't last six months under the same roof.

At two, they were sitting in chairs on the veranda, drinking cool glasses of lemonade, when a car came round the bend and emerged from the trees. 'Ah,' said Bill as he stood up. 'Here's our young couple to inspect the apartment.'

Their names were Gary and Dianne Farland and they were so young and eager and enthusiastic that they made Autumn herself feel old. Somehow, somewhere along the way, she had lost that bright and eager zest for life. And as she groped backward to when it must have happened, she realised that it was when she had given up her secretarial work for modelling. There was something so sophisticated about modelling that it stifled spontaneous enjoyment of the simpler things of life. Not so with the Farlands.

'This place is wonderful!' Dianne sighed as she gazed up at the house. Her long blonde hair, tied back at the nape of her neck, bounced jauntily as she moved her head with quick, birdlike movements. 'We never expected a plantation house! Can you imagine?' she enthused. 'Gary just loves old houses and things. Why, he's to be the history teacher at the high school. And to have a place like this to live ... well, it's just too, too much!'

'We're not living here yet, dopey,' said Gary, attempting to squash his irrepressible wife's zeal.

He was unsuccessful. 'No, but if I know you, we will. And I love it already.' She looked as though she could hardly stand still while she took in her surroundings.

Autumn laughed at them both, finding that she was enjoying herself hugely for the first time in ages. 'You'd better look at the apartment before you make up your minds for good,' she suggested.

As she led the way round the house to the side door that opened directly into the apartment, Gary asked, 'How old is the house?'

'It was built in 1840,' she heard Bill answer. 'And there's been a direct line of Robichauxs living in it ever since.'

'But . . . excuse me, Doc, but didn't you tell me yesterday that Miss McBride is the owner?'

'She is.' There was a hard ring to his voice. 'My aunt, who died recently, left the house to her. But the house-keeper and I still live here as well and my offices are in the wing on the opposite end of the house.'

Autumn sighed as she reached the outer door and turned the key in the lock. She wished it hadn't been necessary to explain her ownership of Bellefleur. It had been a warm, friendly day with Bill, but his voice just now had sounded frozen over like a glacier. Beneath the surface, it was obvious, he still had a great and consuming anger over his aunt's treachery.

She opened the door, then stood back as she waved a hand indicating that the others should enter. 'We'll be waiting for you on the veranda when you've finished looking,' she said quietly.

She headed back towards the front of the house and Bill turned as she drew even with him and fell into step beside her. 'Very considerate of you,' he said, with an unusual touch of praise, 'to let them see it alone so they can make their decision in private.'

She shrugged. 'I just know how I'd feel if it were me.'

'With your husband?' he asked.

She looked at him quickly, but his face was inscrutable. 'Well, certainly,' she said. 'If I had one.'

'You just may have one before you know it,' he said dryly, as he inclined his head in the direction of the drive.

Autumn turned to see what he was looking at and was a bit put out to see Ellis's car sweeping to a stop. She had no choice but to walk out to meet him, but not before she heard Bill, under his breath, singing, 'Here comes the bride ...'

She squared her shoulders in order to ignore him and pasted on a smile of welcome for the other man. 'Good afternoon, Ellis. Isn't it a lovely day?'

They mounted the steps to the veranda, where Bill had returned to sit and she said nervously, 'Excuse me. I'll just go make another jug of lemonade.'

'You don't have to do that for me,' Ellis protested quickly.

'I wasn't,' she said with a quick smile. 'But we've a young couple seeing over Mr George's apartment and I thought I'd offer them some as well. Bill,' she added sweetly, 'will keep you company until I return, won't you?'

Since she knew his only desire when he had returned to the veranda had been to make an unwelcome third rather than a polite host, she felt she had got her own back as he gave her a meaningful glance when she brushed past his chair on her way inside.

She found Bertha up from her nap and in the kitchen. 'I've come to make some lemonade,' she announced to the older woman. 'The young couple are here seeing the apartment and Ellis Naquin is with Bill on the veranda, so go on out and keep them company while I get through in here, will you, Bertha? I want you to meet the Farlands in case they decide to take the apartment.'

'I'll fix the drinks, chère,' Bertha offered. 'After all, you cleaned the kitchen at noon.'

'No. No, I *want* to do it. Go on, Bertha, please,' she urged. 'I ... I kind of think Ellis might need a third party there. I don't think he and Bill like each other very much.'

Bertha chuckled. 'So that's how it is, huh? But how come you don't want to rush back out there to his defence, Automne?'

'Hmph!' Autumn snorted indignantly. 'Bill is saying sarcastic things to me and practically has me married off to Ellis. After one date, mind you! And I will *not* give him further ammunition. Now, will you get going, Bertha?'

The older woman openly laughed. '*Mais* yes, *chère*, I'll go, I'll go.'

A few minutes later when she carried out a tray loaded with icy glasses of lemonade and a plate of cookies, Autumn was relieved to find that the Farlands had joined the others.

'Well, what have you decided about the apartment?' she asked as she offered Dianne a glass.

Dianne accepted the glass and took several cookies. 'We love it, and of course we want to take it. It's just perfect for us ... and that second bedroom is an unexpected bonus which we sure will be needing in a few months.'

Autumn looked blank. 'Are you expecting visitors, then?'

Dianne laughed and her face delicately pinked. 'A permanent visitor—we're expecting a baby. You——' She grew quite serious. 'You will allow us to have a baby in the apartment, won't you? I'm afraid we didn't think to ask before, and some places don't allow children.'

'Why, I'm delighted,' said Autumn with a huge smile on her face. 'Let me be the first to offer my baby-sitting services whenever you and Gary want to go out.'

'Thanks,' Dianne smiled. 'But that's still a long way off.'

'The baby isn't due until the end of January,' Gary put in. 'But we sure appreciate your offer. It'll be great having someone right here who wants to help care for the baby, since both our families live too far away to be of any day-to-day practical help.'

'And me, I'll help with the baby, too,' said Bertha. 'I never had no children of my own, no, but I helped both my sisters to raise theirs. And I helped raise the doctor here, since he was five. It'll be nice to have a baby round here.'

'Thanks, both of you,' Dianne said warmly. 'I was sort of dreading moving here to a small town where we didn't know anyone, but between you, you're already making me feel at home.'

'That's good,' nodded Bertha. And Dr Billy, here, he'll take care of you before the baby gets here, yes?'

Bill grinned and said dryly, 'Drumming up business for me, Bertha? Perhaps they'd prefer going to Houma and finding themselves another doctor. After all, I'm a family practitioner, not an obstetrician.'

'Hmph!' Bertha snorted, leaving no one in doubt of her feelings on that subject. Because she believed that the sun rose and set in her 'Dr Billy', she saw no good reason why others shouldn't appreciate his talents as much as she.

'With a doctor right next door?' Dianne asked in amazement. 'Now why on earth would I want to waste all that time each month driving to Houma and back to see some strange doctor?'

'Yeah,' Gary agreed, 'I figure that's one of the other great benefits of renting this apartment—having a resident physician. We—we're kind of new at all this, you know,' he added nervously, as though it wasn't perfectly apparent to all that this was their first experience with childbirth.

Autumn happened to glance over at Ellis, who was sitting with a bored and slightly embarrassed expression on his face. He had been left out of the conversation most shamelessly. Taking pity on him, she ignored Bill and went to sit instead on the edge of Ellis's chair. It was giving Bill more 'ammunition', which she had told Bertha she was determined to avoid, but it really couldn't be helped. She couldn't bring herself to treat Ellis rudely and make him feel that he should never have come. Beside which, she liked him. She only wanted to avoid serious entanglements.

'I hope you're not getting seriously entangled with Naquin,' Bill said to her the next morning as they went along the connecting hall to the office.

'Why?' she demanded, bristling instantly.

He shrugged. 'Because you just broke with one man in New York before you came here. You don't want to confuse your liking for Naquin with love and marry him on the rebound.'

She lifted quizzical eyebrows at him. 'Are you a psychiatrist?' she asked coldly.

Instead of putting him in his place, which was outside of her personal affairs, she only succeeded in making him laugh. 'You are swift on the uptake, aren't you?' he said with mock admiration. 'Okay, but don't say I didn't warn you.'

'I can handle my own affairs very nicely, thank you,' she retorted.

It was another busy morning and Autumn plunged in. One thing about it, she thought in all fairness, one had to hand it to Bill, he was a good doctor. And a popular one. In the few days she had worked for him she had yet to hear a single person address him formally as Dr Robichaux. The entire population of St Pierre called him Dr Billy, or simply Doc. Even the smallest of children seemed to adore him, although he didn't indulge in any teasing or playfulness or deception. When he was about to hurt a child, he told him or her just what to expect so that the child had no unpleasant surprises. And they appeared to respect him for it. Autumn respected him for it, too. This respect was totally divorced from any personal opinion she might have of him. Which, of course, she told herself, was dislike—at least, sometimes, she amended.

About mid-morning, Pauline Blanchard telephoned. 'Is that you, Miss McBride?' she asked in a smooth, liquid voice. 'I'd like to speak to Bill, please.'

'I'm sorry, but he's rather busy just now, Mrs Blanchard. Would you like to hold or do you want him to return your call?'

'I'll hold,' she said. 'But do tell him at once that I'm on the line.' The last was an order, not a request, and Autumn's temper flared. She clenched her hands and counted to ten before she rose and went down the hall to locate Bill.

He was just emerging from an examining room. 'Oh, Autumn, would you call the hospital in Houma? I'm sending Mr Frank in for an appendicectomy, right away.'

'Yes, Doctor, at once. Mrs Blanchard is on line two waiting to speak to you.'

'Pauline?' His dark eyes narrowed as he looked at her.

'Yes,' she said. And as a parting shot as she turned to leave, she couldn't help adding, 'I hope you're not getting seriously entangled.'

She saw him give a quick smile. '*Touché*,' he said, as he crossed the hall to his private office and scooped up the telephone receiver. Before she could get completely away she heard him saying warmly, 'Hello, Pauline. How are you?'

During the afternoon he had a visitor. 'Hi,' a large, burly man greeted her as he came up to her desk. He was dressed in an obviously expensive pale grey suit, but somehow his very air made it look casual. 'You must be new here,' he told her. 'I haven't seen you before.'

'I'm Autumn McBride,' she said, and added with a smile, 'Yes, I am new here.'

'McBride?' he repeated thoughtfully. 'Oh, you must be that gal who inherited Bellefleur.'

'Yes, sir,' she admitted. 'And now, what can I do for you? Do you have an appointment with the doctor?'

He laughed, and it was deep and rich. 'Now I ask you, do I look sick to you?' he demanded. 'No, I'm a friend of the Doc's. My name's Addie Ledet.' He stuck a cigarette between his lips and lit it before adding, 'Suppose I could see him for a few minutes?'

'I'll check and see,' she said as she rose to her feet. Then she added hesitantly, 'Er ... Mr Ledet, you're not supposed to ... er ... smoke in here.' She pointed to a sign on the wall.

He looked at the sign, back at her, and at the cigarette, as he removed it from his mouth and then laughed and good-naturedly drowned it in the flower vase on her desk.

'Fancy that,' he said musingly. 'My wife would like you. Not many people tell me to put out a cigarette.'

Autumn felt embarrassed, and even more so when Bill suddenly appeared.

'Hi, Addie,' he greeted as the two men shook hands. 'Why

didn't you tell me he was here, Autumn?' he asked almost accusingly.

Addie Ledet said mildly, 'She was about to go for you, Bill, but I lit up a cigarette and she thought it was her duty to tell me to put it out.'

Bill lifted his eyebrows in surprise as he gazed at Autumn's red face. Then he laughed and clasped Mr Ledet's shoulder. 'Good for her! I've told you enough times to give up those filthy weeds.'

Their voices faded as they moved down the hall and into Bill's office.

Autumn completely forgot the little incident until a couple of days later, when one afternoon a dark-haired, very attractive woman who was probably in her late twenties came into the office. She walked briskly across the waiting room, which miraculously, for a few minutes, was entirely devoid of patients.

'Are you Autumn McBride?' she asked in a blunt, yet somehow curiously friendly voice.

'Why, yes,' Autumn answered, 'I am.'

The other woman studied her face thoughtfully. Suddenly she nodded, as though her mind was made up about something. 'I thought so,' she said decisively. 'My husband told me what a beauty you were, so naturally I had to see for myself.'

Autumn felt bewildered, and then the other woman laughed, her voice sounding remarkably like tinkling bells. 'I'm Marianne Ledet. My husband told me you ordered him to put out a cigarette the other day when he visited the office.'

'Oh, no,' Autumn said in dismay, 'I never *ordered* him. I merely *asked* him.'

'Well, I'm glad you did,' said Mrs Ledet. 'I've been nagging him for years to give up smoking and so has Bill, but he ignores us both. Any time anyone can get him to throw away even one cigarette, it's at least one less that he's smoked.' She cocked her head to one side as she studied

Autumn quite openly. 'Yes, Addie was quite right—you are very lovely. I suppose by now that all the single men in St Pierre have fallen in love with you?'

Autumn felt quite taken aback at such an approach. Now she stammered, 'Oh, I don't think . . .'

'But of course they have,' the other woman went on, as though Autumn had not attempted to speak at all. 'At least, those who have met you have. But I imagine Bill Robichaux would have top running, wouldn't he, living in the same house with you and all.' She paused for only an instant before continuing, 'Not that I'm trying to imply anything, you understand. I know Bertha Guidry lives with you and a better chaperone couldn't possibly be had, let me tell you. But still, wouldn't it be romantic if you and Bill were to fall in love with each other? It would be the perfect, fairy-tale ending—the girl being willed the house, the man being willed the property and the two marrying and putting it all together.'

Autumn attempted once more to assert herself. 'I—I assure you, Mrs Ledet, that no such thoughts have . . .'

Marianne Ledet held up a restraining hand. 'But of course not. I can tell at a glance that you're far too nice a person to plot such a thing. And besides, I'm probably getting too far ahead of you, aren't I? Addie tells me I always do. I do try not to, but I just can't seem to help leaping to happy conclusions. I can always see them so clearly for others, you know. Most people can't see the forest from the trees, but I see the forest clearly. And even Addie has to admit that I'm usually right. However, you may have a boy-friend back in—where is it?—New York, isn't it?—so I could just possibly be wrong. Are you already engaged?'

'Well, no, but . . .'

'Great. Then if it's not to be Bill, there are plenty of other single men in the vicinity that we can pair you off with.'

'Oh, I don't think . . .' Autumn tried once again.

'Never mind. It's still early days and we don't want to

push things too fast, do we, now? Much nicer for you to play the field for a while and be a popular flirt.'

'A—a flirt?' Autumn stammered.

'Well, enough of that for now,' the other woman decided. 'I didn't come today to discuss your love life. I came to meet you and to welcome you to St Pierre and to tell you I'm having a dinner party a week from Saturday night for Addie's birthday and though he thinks it's perfectly silly to have birthday parties at his age, he would really be hurt if I didn't give him one, and you absolutely must insist that Bill get to the party, at least for a while, no matter *what* emergency crops up, because Addie will be terribly disappointed if he doesn't come. But I'm assuming you'll have no trouble at all persuading Bill, will you, a lovely girl like you?'

'I . . . I doubt that I could talk Bill into going anywhere, much less insist,' said Autumn, finally getting out an entire sentence. 'I have no influence over him whatsoever, but I'll give him your message and . . .'

'What message is that?' asked Bill from behind her. Autumn almost jumped and could only hope he had just walked in and hadn't had time to hear any of the previous conversation. 'Hello, Marianne,' he added warmly. 'How are you today?'

'Hi, Bill,' the other girl smiled at him. 'I stopped by to remind you about Addie's birthday party a week from Saturday. And I've asked Autumn here to bring you and absolutely accept no excuses. Besides, I'm sure you'll be thrilled to escort such a beautiful girl as Autumn and . . .'

Autumn lost the drift of the remainder of the speech, because she was so horrified—and embarrassed. She hadn't understood that she was being invited, too. Now she cut in rudely upon Marianne Ledet's flow of words, realising it was the only way possible ever to get a word in edgewise. 'I—I appreciate the invitation, Mrs Ledet,' she began, 'but there's no question of Bill taking me. Naturally he'll have other plans and you mustn't assume that he would be free to escort me anywhere just because we happen to share a house.'

Marianne Ledet's sparkling hazel eyes studied her thoughtfully, and then she swung around to Bill. 'And do you,' she asked blandly, 'have other plans for next Saturday night?'

For a moment there was silence, and Autumn was very conscious of Bill's glance upon her. Then he shook his head.

Marianne nodded at him. 'That's fine. Then it's all settled. You'll bring Autumn to our party. We'll see you both then. 'Bye!' With a jaunty wave she breezed out of the office.

Autumn stared down at her hands for the longest time. She dreaded having to meet Bill's eyes. Yet she could feel his eyes again resting on her as he stood beside her.

Finally she faced the inevitable and lifted her head. 'Sorry you've been let in for this,' she said briskly, hoping she sounded amused rather than upset, 'but Mrs Ledet just doesn't allow you to speak long enough to refuse her.'

To her relief, his tone was easy as he replied, 'Better folks than you have attempted it and failed. Marianne Ledet invariably has her own way about everything in this community. But since she has such a kind, generous heart, she gets away with it. Just wait—at the party she'll bring up the subject of some new charitable project she's backing, and before the end of the evening all the guests will have emptied their pockets and purses or volunteered for a job on the project. Probably both.'

'All the same,' Autumn said stiffly, 'it's not fair for her to badger you into taking me to the party when I'm sure you'd rather take someone else. Besides, I don't want to go—I won't know any of the other guests. So come next Saturday evening, I'll conveniently have a headache and then you'll be off the hook.'

His reply was to catch her suddenly by the arm. 'You'll do nothing of the kind,' he said sarcastically. 'I know it'll be hard for a glamorous model like yourself to be paired off for an evening with a fishing bum country doctor, but it won't kill you. I expect you to be dressed and ready to go with me by seven-thirty that evening. Is that clear?'

Before she could possibly form an answer he had turned and gone. Autumn stood rooted to the spot, astounded at his outburst. If she hadn't known better—that there was a certain Pauline Blanchard in the offing—she might *almost* suspect that he actually wanted to take her to the Ledets' party.

And despite her reluctance to go she couldn't help having a tiny quiver of anticipation. But whether it was due to the idea of a party and meeting new people, or due to the fact that she would be going with Bill Robichaux, she wasn't sure. And for some reason she did not care to delve for the answer.

CHAPTER FIVE

'You're up early today,' he observed as, the following Monday, he stood framed in the open kitchen doorway. 'And why are you cooking breakfast instead of Bertha?'

As she looked up, she couldn't help appreciating the picture he made ... dark slacks on long, lean legs, a pale blue dress shirt and a dark blue and white striped tie, all against the glowing bronze of his skin.

'The rain storm that came through early this morning woke me,' she told him. 'I couldn't go back to sleep. And when the storm ended and the sun peeped out I just didn't want to waste time sleeping any more. Bill, do you realise how glorious the courtyard is early in the morning on a summer day? I've decided we're having our breakfast there today.'

'Sounds fine to me,' he replied as he came further into the room. He pointed towards the bowl she held, in which she was beating eggs and asked, 'What can I do to help?'

'Pour yourself a cup of coffee,' she said promptly, 'and sit down. I'll soon have everything ready and then, if you like, you can carry Bertha a tray up to her bedroom. I thought it would be nice to let her have breakfast in bed for a change.'

Her eyes met his and there was a strange look on his face. 'What's the matter?' she asked.

He poured his coffee, sat down and crossed one leg over the other before answering. Then he shrugged his shoulders. 'I don't know what to make of you, sometimes.'

'Meaning?'

He shrugged again. 'You don't look at all the sort to put yourself out to do any work at all, much less to take on someone else's chores and wait on them.'

67

'You've really got some opinion of me, haven't you?' she said hotly.

'That's right,' he agreed easily, 'I have.'

This time it was her turn to shrug. 'Well, if you've already made up your mind, there's nothing more I can do, is there?' Pointedly she turned her back to him and poured the eggs into the hot skillet. 'Feeling as you do,' she added stiffly, 'perhaps you'd better get someone else to do your office work. I'm sure Bertha will pitch in and help out again until you get someone else.'

Two firm hands came down on her shoulders without warning. The heat from them seemed to burn right through the thin cloth and into her skin. Now the hands forced her to turn around until her face was only inches from his.

For a long moment they simply gazed at one another. Autumn held her breath without even being aware of it as the electric moment held her in its grip.

Then an insistent odour penetrated her absorption. 'The ... the eggs!' she gasped. Bill's hands dropped from her arms as she whirled around to rescue their breakfast and the moment was gone.

Autumn had thought for a few breathless seconds that Bill had been about to kiss her, but now he was speaking prosaically of the back kitchen porch steps needing replacing. It must have been a fancy of her imagination.

And anyway, had she *wanted* him to kiss her? And if so, why? Her heart still ached with a dull thud whenever she thought of Don, of the way he had proved to her that he didn't really care about her after all. So why would she want attentions from any other man? Vanity—just to prove to herself that she could still attract men, even though Don didn't want her enough to marry her? No, she didn't think so; she had never been a scalp collector. And besides, what made her think she was really appealing to Bill? He had made it plain enough, numerous times, that he disliked her looks, that he didn't think she could continue pulling her weight when it came to work. That's what the little scene

just now had all been about. So it was stretching the imagination to think that she interested a man like him.

Unconsciously she squared her shoulders, mentally telling herself to forget what had just happened between them.
It had just been one of those odd, breathless little moments
that could seem so important at the time, but in actual fact
meant nothing. She would not read anything into it. Now
she turned and placed the platter of bacon on the table,
conscious of his gaze upon her.

Breakfast in the courtyard was pleasant. Although the
stones beneath their feet were wet, the table and chairs,
which had been covered with canvas, were dry. It was a
lovely rain-washed world. In the yard, the grass, the leaves
on the trees and azalea bushes, were vivid emerald green.
Roses, yellow, white, all shades of pink and red, sparkled
with their diamond water droplets and the air was heavy
with their perfume. The courtyard itself, semi-enclosed by
the house on three sides, was a lush, tropical oasis. Potted
fan-shaped palms concealed corners; huge elephant ears
dominated; ferns and ivies ran riot and clumps of marigolds
in pots provided bright splashes of yellow against their
green backdrop.

'It's heavenly here,' Autumn sighed with deep satisfaction
as she drank in her surroundings. 'You have a wonderful
home, Bill.'

'It's your home too, now. Remember?'

Her gaze went to his face. There was no bitterness in his
eyes now, nor had there been any in his voice. 'You're
right,' she agreed in surprise. 'I keep forgetting.' Then
suddenly she leaned forward. 'I'm sorry. Don't you just
absolutely hate having to share it all with me?'

He shook his head. 'It's not so bad as I first thought it
would be,' he said. His face was inscrutable. 'Not nearly.'

Surprise sent swift colour to her face as she smiled with
pleasure. 'I'm glad,' she said simply. 'I'm really glad.' And
then, before the atmosphere could possibly threaten to become tense again, she stood up. 'It's almost time to go to

the office. I'll carry these dishes back to the kitchen and then I'll join you.'

'Just a moment,' he said, stopping her. Abruptly he turned from her and went out on to the wet lawn. She watched in fascination as he plucked a bright yellow rose and came back to her. He tucked the rose into a buttonhole at the top of her dress. 'It goes with your scarf,' he said.

'Th-thanks,' she stammered out nervously, not knowing what else to say.

'Now go,' he ordered. 'That was just a little thank-you for such a pleasant breakfast.'

'Oh,' she said, suddenly deflated. She picked up the tray of dishes and turned towards the house even as he had already turned towards the door that opened into his offices.

On Thursday, Gary and Dianne Farland began moving into their apartment. Autumn didn't have a moment to spare in greeting them that morning because she was so busy at the office, but at noon she and Bertha had a hurried and agreeable conference in the kitchen.

'I thought you might feel that way,' Bertha told her, 'so I made up a big pot of chicken gumbo, yes.'

'Great,' said Autumn approvingly. 'I'll put together some sandwiches and cut a few slices of your pineapple upside-down cake. That way there'll be enough for their lunch and supper.'

'I thought I'd make a pot of coffee, me,' Bertha added, nodding agreement with Autumn's plans. 'I can pour it up into that big thermos Dr Billy takes with him whenever he goes fishing.'

'Good idea,' Autumn agreed.

When Bill walked into the kitchen a few minutes later and reached for a sandwich on the table, his hand was smartly slapped. 'Those are not for you,' Autumn told him severely. 'They're for the Farlands.'

'What?' he demanded. 'Am I supposed to starve while you women go and feed the neighbours?'

Bertha threw back her head and chuckled. 'Now when have you ever missed a meal when old Bertha was around?' she asked. 'You'll get your dinner, all right. But first, Automne and me, we got to give this food to those young 'uns, yes. That girl, she's eating for two, you know.'

'And that takes top billing over a hungry doctor any day,' Autumn said saucily. It was the first time she had felt on a free and easy basis with Bill since that morning they had had breakfast in the courtyard, a dangerous situation she had not dared to repeat.

'Well, if you're both ranged against me, I guess I'll just have to bow to the inevitable. So,' he added as he picked up the platter of sandwiches, 'let's go and deliver the food. The sooner we do, the sooner we can eat, too.'

'My, but this all looks nice and confused,' Autumn remarked a few minutes later as the three of them stood with the Farlands in their cluttered living room. Cardboard boxes were everywhere; several paintings were propped against the sofa; a bedroom lamp sat in the centre of the floor beside a pile of books.

'It's going awfully slow,' said Dianne. 'But then,' she added with a laugh, 'Gary won't allow me to lift anything that weighs over two pounds. Dr Robichaux,' she appealed, 'will you please explain to my husband that unborn babies and mothers-to-be don't break very easily?'

Bill grinned but shook his head. 'Your husband is only trying to take good care of you, and I'm not going to scold him for that.'

Dianne put her hands on her hips and glared at Bill in exasperation. 'I might have known you men would stick together!' she complained. 'Honestly, sometimes I really believe the only reason Gary wanted this apartment was because of having a doctor in residence only yards away. He's likely to fuss you and me both to death, Doctor!'

As Bill laughed, Gary Farland, with a bit of heightened colour but a good-natured grin, admitted, 'You better believe I'm glad there's a doctor in the house, what with no hospital closer than Houma or New Orleans. But,' and now his gaze swept over Autumn and Bertha, 'I'm also glad the house includes two nice ladies like you. Dianne's mother just hated the idea of us moving to a town where Dianne had no female relatives, especially now while she's expecting, and I told her about how friendly you'd both been the day we came out to look over the apartment and that seemed to relieve her mind a bit.' Now his hand waved towards the food just deposited in the kitchen. 'But I never dreamed you'd be this kind and helpful.'

Dianne smiled. 'Gary's right—we're going to love it here, I know. And now will you all share the dinner with us? How about a bowl of gumbo, Dr Robichaux? That's as soon as I can locate the bowls, of course.'

'No, thanks,' Bill answered. 'Bertha left plenty for us at home. But call me Bill, won't you? Neighbours sharing the same house shouldn't be so formal.'

Dianne gave him a warm smile and as Bill took her hand Autumn felt a twinge of something. Was it envy, bitterness, dislike? She couldn't precisely put a finger on it. She was only aware that somehow the day wasn't quite so bright for her any more and that it was all quite, quite silly. She wouldn't dare allow herself to feel jealous of a sweet young happily married girl just because Bill smiled at her and held her hand for a moment. That was too ridiculous even to contemplate. So what exactly was this feeling she was beginning to have for Bill Robichaux?

But deep inside she really didn't want to ponder it. Maybe she was afraid of what thought would reveal. At any rate, later that afternoon when Ellis Naquin telephoned and invited her out to dinner and a movie, she accepted without hesitation. Here was what she needed—a chance to get out, away from the almost constant presence of Bill Robichaux. A few hours away from him, her work, from the heavy atmosphere of Bellefleur itself, would be just what she needed.

They decided to go to Houma for the evening. It was still

bright daylight as they drove through St Pierre. On the out-
skirts of town, Ellis pointed to another old plantation home,
surrounded, like Bellefleur, by sugar cane fields. 'That's
Pauline Blanchard's plantation now. Used to belong to her
husband's family, but he was the last of the line and there
were no children.'

'Same as the Robichaux family,' Autumn observed
thoughtfully. 'Only Miss Hattie left the place to an outsider
like me instead of to her nephew.'

'That bothers you?' Ellis asked, throwing her a swift
glance.

She nodded. 'Sure it bothers me. I know that morally
Bellefleur belongs to Bill, only ...' Her voice trailed off.

'Only,' Ellis said for her, 'legally it's yours and you like
it and want to stay.'

'Exactly. So ... what should I do?'

Ellis frowned in concentration and for a few minutes was
silent as he passed another car. When they were back in the
right lane again, he said almost harshly, 'It's a ridiculous
situation.' As Autumn stiffened beside him, he realised it
and reached out a hand to pat her. 'Oh, I wasn't criticising
you. If I was criticising anyone, it was Miss Hattie. And not
even her, really. If she hadn't left Bellefleur to you, you
would never have come here and I would never have met
you. Even so, I just can't imagine what she was thinking of
to leave the property so messed up. Obviously you and
Robichaux can't continue sharing a house for the rest of
your lives.'

'And why not?' Autumn asked hotly. 'We have a housekeeper there to make it respectable.'

He looked at her, a bit taken aback by the vehemence in
her voice. 'I only meant that you're both bound to marry in
time,' he explained mildly. 'It's not likely that both your
husband and his wife will want to continue sharing the
house, and what then?'

Somehow Autumn didn't like the thought of that at all.
It was an aspect of the matter to which she hadn't previously

given the slightest bit of consideration. Now she said, just a bit shortly, 'We'll cross that bridge when we get to it.' She glanced out the window at a huge complex of buildings to her right. 'What's that?' she asked, effectively changing the subject.

'That?' He glanced carelessly in the direction she pointed. 'Oh, that's Addie Ledet's sugar refinery.'

'His?'

He nodded. 'His family's. His grandfather started it, I think. Now Addie runs it. Don't know how much longer he'll keep it going—the last one in Houma shut its doors not too long ago.'

'What's the problem?'

He shrugged. 'Higher operating costs,' he told her. 'Foreign competitors, and the fact that more local planters are now going into soybeans instead.'

'Sugar cane is still grown at Bellefleur,' she observed.

Ellis nodded. 'I think Robichaux leases the land to Ledet to farm. They're good friends, you know.'

'I know,' she remarked. 'I met him last week. And his wife, too.'

Ellis looked amused. 'Marianne? I'll bet she talked your ear off, didn't she?'

Autumn grinned. 'She was a bit ... a bit talkative,' she admitted.

'A bit?' Ellis repeated scornfully. 'She's an absolute rattle-trap! Doesn't know when to shut up. If I was Addie, I'd have murdered her long ago.'

'I thought she was very nice,' said Autumn, defending the maligned Marianne. But then she had to admit that she had felt a bit of murder in her heart herself when Marianne had insisted Bill take her to their party this Saturday night. And since that thought still made her a bit nervous, she put it out of her mind and gave herself up to the enjoyment of the evening.

Houma was a fair-sized city, certainly large enough to completely dwarf a small community like St Pierre. Terrebonne Bayou wound its way through the town, just behind the Main Street, while the Intracoastal Canal, on its way towards the Mississippi River, bisected the city, leaving the two sides linked by a tunnel and a drawbridge. Ellis explained to her that a number of bayous snaked their way from Houma down to Terrebonne Bay and, ultimately, the Gulf of Mexico. The swamp area between the city and the Gulf furnished industry for fishermen and trappers alike.

They had a leisurely dinner. Ellis ordered crab while Autumn had shrimp. 'Were these caught locally?' she asked him.

'Probably. You should come in the spring and see the Blessing of the Fleet on Bordeaux Canal. The fishermen come and have their trawlers blessed by the priests before the start of the shrimping season. It's a grand occasion and they all decorate their boats with colourful flags and streamers.'

After dinner they went to a movie. The night air was soft and warm as they drove back to St Pierre late that night, and Autumn was feeling pleasantly drowsy when they arrived back at Bellefleur and Ellis cut the motor of the car. But when he turned towards her, she straightened her shoulders and shook her head. 'Don't, Ellis,' she said softly, forestalling the kiss she knew he had been about to give her. 'Not yet, please.'

'Not yet?' he asked. 'But Autumn, I thought you liked me!'

He sounded so much like a petulant little boy that Autumn couldn't help but laugh gently. 'I do like you,' she told him swiftly.

'But...?' he asked quietly.

'But I'm just not ready to get involved with anyone at this time.' She could tell by the look on his face, which was only illuminated by the moonlight, that he was about to argue the point, so quickly she picked up her bag and, opening the door, slipped out of the car. 'I've enjoyed the evening very much, Ellis. No, don't bother to get out—I can find my way to the door just fine. Goodnight.' And before he could stop her, she ran lightly across the lawn to the house and vanished through the doorway.

On Friday morning Pauline Blanchard came into the office. She looked cool and elegant in a soft blue dress that seemed to float about her rather than constrict her tiny body in any way. Autumn felt at a decided disadvantage in her service-able brown and white striped shirt dress, especially as she towered over the other girl. 'May I help you?' she asked quietly as she looked up from her desk.

'Yes,' Pauline told her in a self-confident voice. 'I'd like to see the doctor, please. On personal business.'

Naturally, Autumn thought. Pauline certainly didn't ap-pear in the least need of the professional services of a doctor. Aloud, she said, 'I'll ring him,' as she picked up the telephone and dialled.

A moment later Bill was coming down the hall, a wel-coming smile on his face. 'Pauline,' he said, coming to take her hand. 'How nice to see you. What can I do for you?'

As he spoke he drew her arm through his and turned her towards the hall and his office. 'I dropped by to see if you're free for dinner tomorrow night,' she said.

Just before they vanished into his private office, Autumn could hear him refusing. 'I'm so sorry, but ...'

Autumn felt disgusted. If Bill wanted to be with Pauline, there was no reason why he shouldn't. After all, he was the one who had insisted that Autumn herself attend the Ledets' dinner party with him. She had a good mind to walk into his office right now and tell him he was perfectly free to have dinner with the other woman; only the ringing of the tele-phone and a new insurge of patients arriving stopped her. And by the time she had another spare moment to think about the matter, she realised how foolish that move would have been. A girl simply couldn't go and tell her boss in front of another woman that she'd be happy to break their date so he could be with the second one. So she waited until Pauline left and the rest of the morning patients had been dealt with. But at noon, after she had locked up the waiting room and turned to see Bill standing over her desk, flipping through the appointment pages for the following week, she tackled him about it at once.

'I would like you to know,' she said in what she tried to make a rather dry, amused voice, 'that you're perfectly free to break your date with me for tomorrow evening.'

He looked up from the appointments book and, beneath the piercing gaze of his dark eyes, her face scalded. 'Am I now?' he all but drawled. 'And may I ask just what gave you the odd notion that I want to?'

'Simple,' she responded quickly. 'I heard you and Mrs Blanchard. So if you . . .'

He cut in on her words in a curt tone of voice she had never heard before. 'Am I to understand that you were *eavesdropping* on our conversation at my office door?'

Her face burned hotter. 'Of course not!' she cried angrily, stung at the suggestion. 'I've certainly got better things to do with my time than to listen at doors!'

'Then how is it that you're in a position to know whether I want to break a date with you in favour of Mrs Blanchard?'

'I merely heard her ask you to have dinner with her before you closed your door, and you refusing. But you don't need to refuse, that's what I'm trying to tell you. You're perfectly free to break our date and take Mrs Blanchard to the Ledets' party instead.'

'I'm afraid I can't do that,' he said in that still freezing voice. 'Marianne specifically invited *you*, not Pauline, remember? So whether I want to be with you or with Pauline Blanchard doesn't enter into it at all. I'll expect you to be ready tomorrow evening at seven-thirty.' He turned his broad back on her and walked away, leaving Autumn feeling slightly battered. She had tried to be generous, offering to release him from their date, but somehow it had ended making her look small and inconsiderate.

The following evening she went down the stairs quaking inside with nervousness. She and Bill had spoken only when business necessitated ever since that awful scene yesterday. Now, as she reached the bottom of the stairs, he stepped out of the library and came slowly to meet her.

He was dressed in a dark suit which emphasised his broad shoulders, his wide chest, his lean legs. The soft hall light played highlights and shadows across the planes of his face and Autumn was struck by his masculine good looks. The sight of him was suddenly doing strange things to her breath and she felt oddly vulnerable, but if she had been asked, she couldn't have explained it for the world.

Their eyes met and his gaze was dark and compelling. For a long moment he held his look before finally his gaze slid away from her face and swept over the long, flowing lines of her lime green dress that so lightly caressed her breasts and hips and thighs. 'You look ... incredibly beautiful,' he said slowly, reluctantly. But the tone of his voice told her that he wasn't saying it in a pleased manner, even before he added, 'You're far too out of place here in a small community like this. You ought to be back in New York beneath the camera lights.'

Somehow his words slashed deeply and, to hide the hurt, she put on a brave and seemingly careless smile. 'It isn't your decision to make, is it?' she pointed out. 'And you're wrong. Everyone else seems to think I belong here. But then,' she added recklessly, 'they don't have a house to gain all to themselves if I go away like you do.'

His eyes darkened like two pools of black ink as his eyebrows lowered ominously. His mouth seemed suddenly chiselled from granite as he said in a hard, controlled voice, 'I think we'd better leave now, don't you?'

Autumn felt slightly ashamed of herself for throwing such rude words at him, but at the same time, he deserved them. He was always running her down, always letting her know at every opportunity that he felt, because of her looks, that she didn't belong, that she should go away, that she could only be decorative like a hothouse flower, a drain on society rather than a contributing member.

The drive to the party was accomplished in silence. The evening, as far as Autumn was concerned, was already ruined. Now she had lost every vestige of interest in the party. She simply wished it was all over so that she could return to her room and be away from the presence of this man at her side.

The Ledets met them at the door and greeted them warmly. 'I *knew* if anyone could drag our doctor away from his work and get him to Addie's party, it would be you!' Marianne exclaimed as she clasped one of Autumn's hands tightly. 'We're so glad to see you both, and everyone is just *dying* to meet you, Autumn. Addie, you must provide Bill and Autumn each with a drink and then Bill can introduce Autumn around, though I think quite a few of our guests have already met her either at church or at Bill's office. I must say ...' As the doorbell rang again, it effectively cut Marianne off in mid-sentence and, with a little push, she propelled Bill and Autumn towards the room behind her.

In actual fact, it was Addie Ledet who introduced Autumn to her fellow guests, not Bill, who trailed behind them more slowly. Autumn sat down on a sofa beside a pleasant-looking lady in black lace who had been introduced as Grace Hebert. As Autumn looked up, she met Bill's eyes across the room and was disconcerted to see that there was a glint of amusement in his eyes. It was almost as though he could read her mind and knew that she had chosen to sit here where there was no space for him to sit beside her.

Abruptly she lowered her eyes and concentrated her attention on the woman next to her. She soon learned that Mrs Hebert was the high school home economics teacher and a recent widow and that this was her first social event since her husband's death eight months ago. 'I really didn't feel like coming here tonight,' she confided to Autumn in a low voice that couldn't possibly carry. 'I feel so out of place, somehow. But you know what Marianne is. She simply wouldn't take no for an answer.'

Autumn laughed in sympathy. 'I know very well what you mean.'

They chatted on easily, and by the time they went in to dinner, Grace Hebert had extracted a promise from Autumn to come to the high school and speak to her teenage girls about her modelling career and its related subjects of proper nutrition, exercise and rest, as well as choosing proper clothes and make-up.

It was after dinner that Autumn's blood sizzled to the surface again. All the guests were lounging once more in the roomy, modern living room with its red brick fireplace, which had a wicker basket bouquet of bright yellow and orange zinnias in its grate. Autumn was listening to Mayor LeCompte's account of a recent visit to Europe when, during a lull in the conversation behind her, she heard someone say, 'You sure are a lucky devil, Bill, to have a beautiful girl like Autumn to move down here and live in your home.'

For the life of her Autumn couldn't help looking around just as Bill replied easily, 'Yes, I am lucky. Very lucky.' As though perfectly aware that she was watching him, he looked straight across at her, his lips stretched into a sardonic grin as he lifted his glass towards her in a taunting salute.

Pain stabbed through her and swiftly she turned away, unable to bear his cruelty any more. For some reason it hurt unbearably that he could joke and make fun of her that way. And to hide the unexpected hurt, even to herself, she whipped up the flames of anger. Somehow anger was an easier emotion to deal with, certainly a protective emotion. One didn't lose one's pride with anger.

So, by the time they were once again in his car and driving home through the softly caressing Louisiana night, she was hard put to it to answer his slightest remark with anything even approaching civility.

After she had given one or two curt answers to his conversational questions, he lapsed into silence, and Autumn was glad. If he forced her to talk very much, her feelings were bound to come out. She had never been very good at hiding her emotions.

Back at Bellefleur, Bill drove the car into the garage and once they were outside, when Autumn would have made for the back kitchen door, he placed hard, detaining fingers around her arm. 'Let's walk around to the front,' he said in a low voice. 'There seems to be something we need to get straight between us.'

Autumn didn't answer, but she went with him all the same. It would have been undignified simply to jerk her arm from his touch and run, besides showing herself up as a coward. So, with an inward sigh of nervousness, she went with him, hoping the darkness of the night would help to shield what she didn't want him to see.

They were standing in the dark, secretive shadows of the veranda, facing the wide expanse of lawn, side by side but not touching. For a few tense moments there was silence, then he said, 'Something is wrong, and I want to know what it is.'

'And if I don't choose to tell you?' she flung at him.

She could feel his gaze on her, even in the protective darkness. 'Then I'll guess we'll just have to spend the night out here,' he said calmly as he folded his arms and leaned back against the railing. 'Because I intend to know what's wrong before we go inside. You're as bristly as a porcupine.'

Autumn sucked in a deep breath. 'All right, then,' she said in a shaky voice. 'If you must know, I don't enjoy being the object of your sarcastic jokes, that's all.'

At that his hand shot out to grip her wrist tightly and to pull her around so that now they were facing each other. 'What sarcastic jokes?'

'As if you didn't know,' she said scornfully. 'You know as well as I do that when you told that man you were indeed a—quote—"very lucky devil"—unquote—because I moved into your home you were really making fun of me.'

'I wasn't making a joke,' he said evenly.

'Don't make me laugh!' she snapped angrily. 'I wasn't born yesterday. After all, I'm quite well aware of how you feel about me.'

'Yes?' he said. 'Tell me.'

She answered promptly. 'You've disliked me ever since I arrived. You consider me to be a basically useless person because of my looks and the only reason you're civil to me at all is because I do have a legal right to be here and so you consider yourself obliged to be somewhat polite since we actually share the same house.'

'Have you quite finished all you have to say on the subject?' he demanded harshly when she paused for breath.

Surprised at the note of anger in his voice, she nodded. And then his arms were round her and her body was pulled close to his until her face was only inches from his own. With patent anger, he bent his head until his lips laid siege to hers. It was a kiss that seemed to have no beginning and no end. It simply was an entity of its own, as they stood so close together that the single shadow of their merged bodies blended with the soft darkness of the veranda.

At last Bill lifted his head. His eyes, even in the darkness of night, had a certain intense brightness to them as he looked at her. 'As long as I must be civil to you,' he said softly, 'then I want to be *very* civil.' She continued to gaze at him in a bemused fashion, but before she could begin to unravel his words and attempt to make any sense of them, the porch light flared to life, stripping away the gently covering blanket of the night.

He withdrew his strong, supportive arms from around her, leaving her suddenly chilled despite the warmth of the night, just as Bertha opened the heavy front door and peered out.

'Is that you, Dr Billy?' she called.

'Yes, Bertha. Autumn and I were just enjoying the night air before coming in,' he said in the calmest of voices, as though the emotional upheaval he had just put Autumn through had meant not the slightest to him.

'Well, I hate to interrupt you, yes,' said Bertha, 'but Mrs Blanchard, she called and said she needs you to stop in and see her tonight.'

Bill nodded curtly and moved swiftly across the veranda to the steps. 'I'll go along at once.'

A dull ache spread within Autumn as she followed Bertha inside the house. Bill had dropped her like the proverbial hot potato the minute Pauline Blanchard beckoned. It just went to show once again, if she still needed showing, that men just couldn't be trusted. None of them. They were all simply out for what they could get—from any and all willing females. Once more she felt betrayed, and as she trailed upstairs to prepare for bed, a big lump lodged in her throat.

CHAPTER SIX

THE sun was already high in the sky by the time Autumn awoke the next morning. Sunbeams danced jauntily across the sheets and over her sleep-flushed face. She rolled over to peer closely at the clock, then sat upright in surprise. It was almost nine-thirty—the very latest she had slept in a long time.

But then came the reason for such an unheard-of happening. Bill had not come cheerfully pounding on her door this morning before entering with her coffee. The door remained stolidly closed and the house held only the hushed silence typical of a Sunday morning.

She lay back against the pillows, frowning. There might be a number of explanations to account for Bill's absence. He might have been called out early by a patient, though usually when that happened she heard the bell of the telephone, or perhaps after last night, he simply no longer wanted to awaken her. It might be that he thought, if he continued to do so, she might misconstrue his intentions towards her.

Her fingers went up and almost wonderingly flitted across her soft pink mouth as the rest of her face flamed with embarrassment. Her response to Bill's kiss last night had been as unexpected to her as the kiss itself. It had shaken her to her very soul. In fact, it had affected her far more than any kiss she had ever received from any man before, including Don. And what if Bill had realised that? If that were so, no wonder he didn't want to come around her. He had given way to a momentary impulse and now he regretted it. It must mean that he had no wish for her to read anything serious into his kisses, and so he had seized upon the opportunity to rush away from her and go to the woman he loved and planned to marry as soon as she beckoned.

Autumn piled out of the bed and rushed to the shower, hoping to wash away the hot shame that seared her every time she thought of that throbbing response she had had to Bill's kiss. It had felt so warm and wonderful there in his arms—even now she quivered at the memory of it. But then she drew her wayward thoughts up short. The kiss had meant nothing to Bill: she must, she absolutely must remember that. Bill Robichaux belonged to another woman, his kiss had been a mere whim of the moment, and she would do well to keep those facts to the forefront of her mind if she wanted to avoid being hurt. And something warned her that if she didn't watch it, didn't hold her emotions in strict control, it was possible for her to become very hurt indeed. And to dwell on the possible reasons for such a happening, her mind absolutely refused to do this fine Sunday morning.

She towelled herself dry and returned to her bedroom to dress. There was still plenty of time until the eleven o'clock Mass. As she pulled the sheer honey-toned pantyhose up over her long, slender legs, a vision of Bill's face rose up in her mind despite her resolve to banish all thoughts of him. On previous Sundays she had attended the early Mass with him, but today going to the late service all alone would be quite different. Somehow it took a certain sparkle out of the day.

Which was ridiculous. If she were reaching a state where Bill's mere presence was required for her enjoyment of any given day or event, then things had reached a sad pass indeed and she was going to have to take a strong grip on herself. She would not, *would not* allow him to become that important in her life.

There was an overpowering silence about the house as she went down the stairs and into the kitchen a few minutes later. Bertha had told Autumn the previous day that she would be away all day visiting some cousins on Grand Isle. There was no sound at all from the Farlands' apartment either, because they had gone to New Orleans to visit their families. And Bill was obviously nowhere on the premises. Without even his patients coming and going down the drive, the place was almost eerily quiet.

It was with a sense of relief that she finally set out on foot down the drive after a quick breakfast of coffee and sweet roll. For all she had come to love Bellefleur, Autumn discovered that she didn't at all like the oppressive silence of the house when it was unpeopled by anyone except herself. Alone, it suddenly became gigantic, mysterious and secretive instead of warm and friendly and mellow with age.

Now that she was across the wooden bridge that spanned Bayou Cache, she laughed at her flight of fancy. Mysterious and secretive indeed! Bellefleur was the same house as it was when filled with people. It was only her jumpy nerves that made it seem so different.

She arrived at the church and smilingly responded to several greetings from other members of the congregation as she went inside. And during the next hour she relaxed as she drank in the beauty of the church and the inspiration she needed.

Outside once again, as she walked down the sidewalk through the throng of parishioners who were clustered in friendly little circles, chatting with one another, she suddenly heard her name, and turned to see Ellis Naquin pushing his way through the crowd, coming towards her. When he reached her, he smiled broadly. 'I don't believe my good luck,' he said with obvious pleasure. 'It's so nice to see you.'

Autumn smiled, too. 'It's nice to see you, too, Ellis.'

Ellis's father joined them now. 'How are you, Miss McBride?' he asked as the two of them shook hands.

'I'm just fine, Mr Naquin,' she answered. 'Isn't it a glorious day?'

'It certainly is,' he agreed. 'We'd better enjoy our days like this, because pretty soon the weather will be turning cool.'

'What are you plans for the day, Autumn?' Ellis asked.

'Plans?' she repeated, slightly puzzled. 'No plans.'

'Great,' he said. 'Then why don't you come home with Dad and me for Sunday dinner? Later we can go horseback riding—that is, if you'd like to.'

'Yes, do,' Mr Naquin seconded promptly. 'I must say it would be very nice to have a lovely young lady to grace our table.' He smiled rather wistfully. 'My wife died some years ago and except for our housekeeper we're a womanless house, which gets quite dull sometimes. We'd love to have you, my dear.'

After a moment's hesitation, Autumn smiled and responded to his obviously sincere invitation. 'I'd love to,' she said quite definitely. It would be an enjoyable afternoon and would certainly keep her away from the empty house, so that by the time she did get home, probably either Bill or Bertha would have returned.

'Excellent,' said Ellis with satisfaction as he reached out and took her hand in his. 'Did you drive or walk?'

'I walked.'

'Good. Then you can come along with us now,' he said.

'I'll need a change of clothes,' she reminded him as she looked wryly down at her emerald green dress and jacket. 'I mean, if I'm to ride with you.'

Ellis laughed as he placed a hand possessively on her elbow and began to guide her to the parking lot. 'All right, we'll drive you home long enough for you to pick up some jeans.'

Once the car slid to a halt in the drive in front of the house, Ellis leaned over the seat to open the door for Autumn. 'Don't be long,' he admonished.

'I won't,' she promised with a little wave to both men, who remained in the car. Then she turned and hurried up the steps and into the house.

She was halfway up the stairs when the door to the library suddenly opened. She halted on the staircase and half turned, peering down over the polished wooden banister.

Bill stood framed in the open doorway, gazing up at her. He was dressed in black slacks and a white, casual turtleneck shirt that highlighted the midnight darkness of his hair, his thick eyebrows and the bronze tone of his skin. There was something about his virile good looks that seemed oddly overpowering, and then his face broke into a warm smile that caused Autumn's heart suddenly to flip over. And in that instant she knew why she had been so hurt last night when he had left her to go to Pauline Blanchard. She knew why his kiss had affected her the way it had. She knew why, even now, at this very moment, the sight of him did crazy flip-flop things to her heart. She was purely and simply in love with him.

But how in the world could it have happened without her being aware of it? Did love sneak up unawares like this? She had thought she disliked him, and yet all the time she was falling in love with him and hadn't even realised it. Now she sucked in a deep, quivering breath and gripped the banister rail tightly, as though the sledge-hammer blow of her sudden knowledge might knock her down.

He was still looking up at her with a curious little smile playing across his lips. 'Good morning,' he greeted her.

'G-good morning,' she got out huskily.

'How did you sleep last night?' he asked. She wondered whether she saw just a glint of humour in his eyes.

'Very well, thank you,' she lied, since she had lain awake for long hours thinking of him. However, she had no intentions of admitting that fact to him. But now she couldn't help adding, 'And you?'

He grinned. 'I had the very dickens of a time getting to sleep, myself.'

'Oh? Yes?' Her voice was carefully non-committal.

'Yes. I kept thinking about a certain young woman.'

'And how *is* Mrs Blanchard?' she asked coldly.

The smile left his face. 'We won't discuss her, if you don't mind,' he ordered in a decisive voice. 'Now,' he went on, altering the tone of his voice considerably, 'how would you like to come with me and spend the rest of the day in New Orleans? I'll show you all the sights and then I'll take you to dinner in the French Quarter.'

Autumn felt like bursting into tears. It was all too much, discovering her love for Bill, and now receiving his enticing invitation for her to spend the day with him, while Ellis and his father waited for her outside in the car. She could scream with frustration. Why, why had he asked her today of all days?

She lowered her head so that her eyes wouldn't have to continue meeting his. 'I'm sorry,' she mumbled softly, 'but I can't. I . . . I've made . . . other plans.'

'What other plans?' he asked now in a sharp voice.

'I . . . I . . . the Naquins have invited . . . invited me to have dinner with them. And to go horseback riding. That . . . that's why I came home . . . to pick up a change of clothes.' She realised her words were coming out jerkily and hesitatingly, as though she were admitting to some wrong, and it angered her that it was so, yet she couldn't help it.

His disapproval emanated across the very air until she could feel it almost as though it were a physical touch. 'You'd prefer to go out to the Naquins' place rather than go to New Orleans with me?' he asked in a marble-hard voice.

She raised her eyes again and was instantly wretched at seeing the frost in his. 'I didn't say that,' she told him in an almost pleading voice. 'But I've already accepted their invitation. They're waiting for me now.'

'They're here?'

'Yes,' she nodded unhappily. 'They brought me home so I could pick up some jeans for riding.'

His eyes seemed to pierce hers. Even from a distance of several feet away, his gaze was compelling. 'Are you getting serious about him?' he demanded.

'Ellis?' she asked, almost in a daze. 'No, of course not.'

'He is about you,' he stated unequivocally. 'Do you really think it's fair to encourage him if you don't feel the same way?'

'I ... I don't know what you mean,' she said in a low voice.

'Yes, you do,' he grated out harshly through clenched teeth. His words were sharp-pointed darts. 'Don't play the little innocent! Any girl as beautiful as you are knows all there is to know about how men will make fools of themselves over you. And there must have been plenty. Do you keep a record of how many men fall in love with you?'

Instantly she was blazingly angry. Her eyes glittered like hard, bright diamonds. 'Don't be any more obnoxious than you can help!' she hissed furiously. 'Thank God I do have this date with Ellis, otherwise I might have made the mistake of going with you to New Orleans and spending a dreadfully boring afternoon!'

His eyes glinted like sunlight hitting steel. 'You didn't seem to consider me so very boring last night,' he reminded her. 'But then that was just all part of a game with you, wasn't it? My kisses then—today, Naquin's. Do you tally them up, too?'

Her hand on the banister knotted into a tight fist. 'I ... I hate you, Bill Robichaux!' she exclaimed breathlessly.

He gave her a mocking smile before, without another word, he turned back into the library and very, very gently shut the door behind him, while she stood looking after him, rooted to the stairs.

She was hard put to it to pay adequate attention to her hosts that afternoon. Instead of Mr Naquin's kindly face, she saw Bill's dark, scowling one. In place of Ellis's mouth, were Bill's lips, stretched into a hard, disapproving line. Instead of polite conversation, she was hearing again Bill's harsh, cruelly taunting words. And underlying it all was her newly discovered and completely hopeless love for him in the face of his obvious dislike for her. The hurt of it all was almost too much to bear.

She hadn't ridden horseback in several years and now all her eager anticipation and enjoyment was eroded as she thought of how, if things had been different, she might be seeing the sights of New Orleans with Bill at her side. For all she'd told Bill to the contrary, she was truly wildly disappointed.

'Do you think this is a good spot, or should it be further back among the trees?'

With a jolt, Autumn brought herself into the present. She and Ellis had been riding for some time, but she had been lost in a fog of unhappy thoughts. Ellis had reined in the bay, so now she did the same to the appaloosa and tried to appear alert and interested. 'What did you say?' she asked crisply. 'I'm afraid I was lost in admiration of the view.'

Ellis slid from his saddle and came forward to help her down. 'Let's walk a bit,' he said. As his hand retained its hold upon the waist, Autumn moved away from him and walked over towards a weeping willow as though to examine it closer.

As she touched the tree's drooping greenery, Ellis came to stand beside her, closer than she liked. 'I was asking you if you like this spot for the house I plan to build,' he told her, 'or if you think it should be further back among the trees.'

Autumn shrugged. 'That's not really my decision to make,' she answered. 'That's for you to decide. And your wife if you had one.'

'I agree,' he said as he gazed into her eyes with a disturbing seriousness. 'That's why I want your opinion. Haven't you guessed by now, Autumn?' he asked gently. 'Haven't you guessed that I'm in love with you and that I want you to be my wife?'

'Oh, no!' she exclaimed in dismay.

'Oh, yes,' he corrected with a smile. 'Surely it's not such a surprise as all that? You've known since the very first that I was attracted to you.'

'Yes,' she agreed, lowering her eyes to her hands. 'But I never dreamed that you ... I ... Ellis, we haven't known each other very long at all!'

'That's true,' he agreed. 'But it doesn't take very long to fall in love.'

She was about to argue that point when she realised that what he said was true. It didn't take long. She hadn't known Bill any longer than she had known Ellis and look what had happened to her! Now she sighed and looked up, dreading to have to hurt Ellis.

She licked her lips and plunged in. 'Ellis, I ... I'm sorry. I wouldn't have had this happen for anything in the world. But I ... I just don't love you.'

'It's early days yet,' he said quickly. 'I won't rush you, if only you'll say I have a chance. If you just won't close your mind on the subject.'

She smiled unhappily and shook her head. 'I ... I can't tell you that, Ellis. I *do* like you enormously, but ...' Her voice trailed off miserably.

'You're in love with someone else?' he asked now, as though the possibility had only just occurred to him.

'Yes,' she whispered as her head drooped.

'Someone in New York,' he said gloomily. 'And does he return your love?'

She shook her head, glad at least that he hadn't guessed the truth. 'No,' she admitted reluctantly, 'he doesn't.'

Ellis smiled at her, a smile of sympathy as he reached out and took her hand into his. 'We're in the same boat, huh?' he said shrewdly.

'I ... I suppose so,' she admitted slowly. She looked up at him and began, 'Ellis, I ...'

'I know,' he told her sadly. 'You're sorry—so am I. But it doesn't change things, does it? Tell you what—let's just drop the subject. Who knows, maybe in the future you'll find you do return my love, after all.' Before she could protest, he went on, 'If this man you love doesn't love you, and he must be crazy not to, in my opinion, then maybe later on you'll find out he doesn't matter to you after all. Maybe you'll find out I do. So I'll just hang around and wait and see. Okay? Just as an interested friend and bystander.'

Very soberly they rode back to the stables and then walked across the magnificent lawn with its magnolias, camellias, azaleas, crêpe myrtles and dogwoods to the house where they rejoined the elder Mr Naquin in late afternoon coffee.

Bill was not at home when Autumn returned around six. Bertha hadn't come in yet, either, so Autumn made herself a sandwich and a glass of tea and carried it upstairs to her room on a tray. There she fiercely concentrated on a novel which she hoped would be of such fascinating interest that it would blot out all the revelations of the day.

And what a day it had been—discovering her love for Bill and being told of Ellis's love for herself! Oh, why was life so unfair? Why couldn't life flow easily, with herself returning Ellis's love? It would all be so simple if only she did.

She contemplated marrying Ellis with the hopes of falling in love with him and out of love with Bill after the wedding. In novels, girls were always falling in love with a husband they had married for other reasons. And she was sure that Ellis would make a fine model of a husband and father.

She sighed and closed the book, giving in to the fact that she hadn't taken in a single word of it, though she'd been flipping the pages for some time. The fact was that this was reality, and reality told her that marriage without a mutual love simply wasn't for her, no matter how nice a person her partner was. With her it was all or nothing, and unfortunately it seemed she was stuck with nothing. First she had thought herself in love with Don and had been hurt by the fact that he wanted to live with her and make love to her without benefit of marriage. Then she had to discover what real love was—with a man who most of the time didn't even seem to like her. To top it all off, she had to be loved by a man whom at best she could only be fond of.

Her disobedient thoughts returned again to Bill, to the warmth of his lips on hers—and to his hastening away from her to Pauline Blanchard's side. With a lump in her throat that felt as though it was to be lodged there permanently, she flipped off the bedside lamp and lay staring at the ceiling, knowing it would be hours yet before she could sleep.

Both Bertha and Bill returned home late that night, but late as it was, Autumn heard them. In actual fact, it was closer towards dawn before she fell at last into a restless sleep.

For the next couple of weeks she was aware of a definite constraint between herself and Bill. She worked with him in the office as usual with deceptive ease, but during non-working hours, at home, she did her best to stay out of his way. Which was relatively easy. She was out a lot with Ellis and Bill went his own way. And when she did chance to be at home with him, quite often one of the Ledets or the Farlands dropped in to visit.

The weather turned sharply cool and rainy, and the heavy grey days exactly fitted Autumn's mood. She donned raincoat and galoshes and took long tramps down by the bayou's edge. There, the murky water that moved sluggishly along seemed a perfect duplicate of her humour—foul and black.

One Friday evening in October, the Farlands invited her and Bill to attend a local high school football game. Gary was assistant coach to the team, so of course would not be able to sit with them, but they would be able to keep Dianne company if they went along.

That was the only reason Autumn agreed to go. She liked Dianne a great deal and she supposed Bill must feel the same way. And she supposed he, like herself, must have resolved to bury his feelings for the evening and do his best to give Dianne a good time. Whatever the reason, the tension that had been there so strongly between them for the past weeks seemed to evaporate right into thin air.

Dianne was in bouncy spirits, cheering loudly for the St Pierre Pirates, and Autumn thought with amusement that if it hadn't been for her condition she would have been right down there in front showing the cheer-leaders how to turn a proper cartwheel.

When it became apparent to Dianne that her two companions were not doing their loyal part for the team, she frowned and scolded, 'What's the matter with you two bumps on a log? If the Pirates lose, it'll be all your fault for not helping to cheer them to victory.'

'Our fault?' Bill queried.

'Definitely your fault,' Dianne said firmly. She turned on Autumn. 'Don't you *know* the cheers?' she demanded, suddenly anxious. 'Didn't people cheer at football games in New York?'

Autumn broke into a giggle. 'You make it sound as though I come from Mars, Dianne! Of course we cheered at football games. In fact, I used to *be* a cheer-leader!' she added for good measure.

Dianne looked at her assessingly. 'Yes? Well then, you have absolutely no excuse for sitting here with a zipper on your mouth, do you? And you, Bill,' she exclaimed, swinging around to him. 'I'll bet you used to be a football player.'

'Well, yes,' Bill admitted. 'In fact, I played with the Pirates here, but . . .'

'But you think it's beneath the dignity of a doctor to cheer for his own team?' she demanded. She snapped her fingers. 'That,' she said dismissively, 'for your doctor dignity!'

Autumn burst into laughter at Dianne's indignant demeanour and all at once her eyes met Bill's. For a long moment she held his gaze, and the world suddenly seemed to stand still. Then Dianne made some casual remark and Bill withdrew his gaze from Autumn to answer their friend who sat between them, but somehow Autumn felt that the barrier between herself and Bill had been broken.

The Pirates won over the Warriors ten-seven. Naturally it called for a victory party. The teenagers chose as their hang-out a local pizza parlour and Gary Farland suggested they go there for their refreshments, too.

The restaurant was jumping with loud jukebox music and the excited hum of conversation. The four of them squeezed through the throng of students, looking for an empty booth, an impossible quest. But just as they were on the point of giving up, a group at one booth stood up to leave and one of the boys beckoned to Gary. 'Here, Mr Farland, you can have our table.'

Dianne and Gary slid into one of the booths so that Autumn and Bill were left to do the same on the opposite side of the table. A waitress came and took their orders for Cokes and pizza and as she departed, Autumn was sharply aware of the man at her side. His shoulder brushed hers and the slight touch sent a shiver of exquisite pain through her. Dianne and Gary were openly holding hands across the table, just like the teenagers around them, and Autumn wished she could slip her hand into Bill's.

But of course she couldn't. He turned abruptly to her. 'I feel like a kid again tonight, Miss McBride,' he whispered as he leaned over towards her. 'What about you?'

'Yes, Doctor Robichaux,' she agreed. 'About seventeen.'

'But I'm luckier now than I was then,' he observed. 'I never had a date with such a glamorous beauty when I was in high school.'

Autumn was still lost in a state of enchantment when they returned home. As they went inside, she wondered if Bill would crown the golden evening they had shared with a kiss.

The telephone in the library rang, discordantly jarring both the still silence of the night and her churning thoughts. With a sigh, Bill said, 'I'll get it. It's probably a patient.'

Autumn took over locking the front door and checking the back kitchen door. Bill called out from the library, 'It's for you, Autumn—long-distance.'

She moved across the room and took the receiver from his outstretched hand. 'H-hello?' she said uncertainly.

'Autumn!' the voice exclaimed in a strident, angry tone. 'I want to know who that man is who answered the telephone. When I asked him if he lived there he said yes, but you told *me* you wouldn't live with any man without marriage. What the hell does this mean?'

It was Don! Autumn all but reeled beneath the impact of his furious onslaught of words. Without thinking, she automatically began defending herself. 'I am *not* living with a man,' she said in a rush, 'He's living with me. That is ... he lives in the same house but not *with* me. I mean,' she added desperately, as she realised that her explanation was becoming muddled, 'he's a doctor and he has his offices in this house. And besides,' she ended stiffly, suddenly remembering the circumstances, 'I don't owe you any explanations at all. Resentfully she glanced in Bill's direction. He stood near a window, hands thrust into his pockets and with an interested expression on his face. Why on earth didn't he leave? Surely he realised that this was a private call.

But he went on standing there and, flustered, Autumn tried to force all her attention on what Don was saying on the other end of the telephone wires.

'Darling!' Don's furious voice had altered to tender entreaty. 'Don't be angry,' he pleaded. 'But naturally I'm upset at having a man answer your telephone and tell me he's living in your house. But if you tell me that it's all innocent, then of course I believe you. And I know you don't owe me any explanation—not after what I said to you the last time we met. But I was hurt and angry when I said those things. Of course I didn't get any other girl to come and live with me. How could I, when I'm so in love with you?' He paused, as though expecting some reply on her part, but when she remained stonily silent he went on quickly, filling the breach. 'Darling, I miss you. I want you so much. Will you stop this foolish way of punishing me and come home and marry me?'

'I'm not punishing anybody,' she said stiffly. 'And I have no intention of going back and marrying you.'

'Autumn, I apologise on bended knees! You must forgive me! I know you can't have stopped loving me this soon. Not when I love you so much! Now please be sensible, darling. Sell off that house Joyce told me you'd inherited and come back to me where you belong.'

'I'm sorry, Don,' she said firmly, 'but I intend to stay here.'

'You're still angry with me,' he accused. 'You won't forgive me.'

'I forgive you,' she said in a flat voice.

'Then come home and marry me.'

'No.'

'Then I'll let you have a little more time to get over your anger,' he said indulgently. 'But I warn you, I'm coming down there to your swamps at Christmas, and when I do I intend to put my ring on your finger and bring you back home with me where you belong, so you'd better make your mind up to it.'

'Don't do that,' she said quickly, appalled at the idea of him here in this house, with Bill standing around looking at them as an interested spectator, as he was now. 'Don't come, Don,' she said urgently. 'It would be a complete waste of time.'

'We'll discuss it at Christmas when I see you,' he said lightly. 'Goodbye for now, darling.' Then he hung up before she could protest further.

After a moment she dropped the receiver back into its cradle and then, sputtering furiously, she turned on Bill like an aroused wildcat. 'You've got a damn nerve!' she snapped. 'Listening in on a private conversation! You *knew* you should have gone away!'

'Yes,' he admitted easily, 'but your calls seem so much more interesting than mine.'

She glared at him. She was so enraged she was trembling. She couldn't think of anything cutting enough to say to him, so at last she whirled round and ran across the hall and up the stairs.

Bill followed. 'Who was he, anyway?' he asked as he dogged her footsteps. 'An old flame? The one you left in New York when you came here?'

'Yes,' she snapped. 'Not that it's any of your ...'

'And he's coming here?' he asked in a curiously insistent voice.

'So he says,' she admitted, shrugging indifferently.

'When?'

'Christmas.'

'To marry you?' By now they had reached the landing on the stairs and Bill's hand shot out and gripped her wrist, effectively halting her headlong flight. 'To marry you?' he asked again as they stood facing each other.

She shook her head, feeling slightly breathless. 'Not a chance.'

His eyes narrowed as they searched her face. 'Positive?'

'Yes.' Her voice was crisp, decisive.

He released his tight grip on her arm at last. 'Good,' he said, equally crisp. 'It makes my own position in the house so much more secure.'

'What—what do you mean?' she asked hesitantly.

His smile was mocking. 'It means that I can go on living with you, of course.'

Her face scalded and she snapped angrily, 'You've got a legal right to go on living here whether I marry or not.'

'True,' he agreed readily, 'but it wouldn't be nearly so appealing, your having a husband around cluttering up the place. I don't think,' he added pensively, 'that I'd like sharing this house with another man.'

Autumn drew herself up and tried to look complete mistress of the situation, though she felt she failed miserably. 'You don't happen to have any choice in the matter of whom I marry. Or when I'll marry,' she said with an attempt at dignity.

For reply, he ran a finger down her cheek. 'We'll see,' he said. 'We'll see.'

Then he went past her and on up the stairs, leaving her to wonder exactly what he had meant.

CHAPTER SEVEN

NOVEMBER arrived, nasty and wet and cold. In the office they saw a huge influx of colds and 'flu and bronchial congestions. It kept Autumn busy, having a waiting room filled with patients, and she was glad of the work that kept her on the move. The less time she had to herself, the less time there was to dwell on personal problems.

For the most part she was able to keep her newly discovered love for Bill submerged beneath the ocean of day-to-day concerns. As long as she was busy, even though she had to work with him in the office, she could forget him as a person and deal with him only as her employer.

The problem was a bit more complicated during off work hours, but even that she had pretty much managed to control. Once a week, on Thursday afternoons when the office was closed, she went to the St Pierre High School and spent a pleasant hour with Grace Hebert and the home economics class. Autumn had never had much dealings with teenage girls since she had left her teen years herself, but now she found she had a natural affinity with them. She enjoyed seeing the girls work at good grooming, some to wash off layers of make-up so that their natural glowing skin surfaced, others to discover how to carry themselves proudly, still others to discover the magic that proper diet could work in their looks. A few of the girls had seen Autumn's photograph in magazine advertisements, which to them placed her in the realm of celebrities and which only added to her allure.

Marianne Ledet had unwittingly helped Autumn, too, in her desire to fill up her free time to overflowing. Marianne was chairwoman of St Joseph's Ladies' Aide Society and she easily persuaded Autumn to become an active member.

So one evening a week, along with the other members, Autumn went to the church kitchen to help cook mountains of food which was then distributed to the elderly and ill members of the community.

She was conscious that, if Bill was aware of her efforts to avoid his company, he gave no indication of it. In fact, he scarcely gave any indication at all of being aware of her as a person these days except for that brief moment each morning when he pounded on her door before bringing up a cup of coffee. Autumn, despite all resolve to keep Bill from her mind and her heart, relished those few moments each morning, hugging them to herself as though they were something tangible. If she were heading for heartbreak, then so be it, but at least she would have this much of Bill that belonged only to herself.

She still saw Ellis often. He had kept his promise and their relationship was strictly on a friendship level, the only way that she would continue to see him.

One evening she was waiting downstairs for Ellis to arrive to take her to dinner, but when the doorbell rang, she went to answer it and was startled to find Pauline Blanchard at the door instead.

For a moment they gazed at one another wordlessly. Then Pauline's eyes flickered with some private amusement. 'May I come in?' she asked. 'It's rather cold outside.'

'Oh,' Autumn said blankly. 'Oh, yes, please do.' She stepped back so that the other woman could enter, then she led the way into the little-used front parlour and Pauline said from behind her, 'I came for Bill.'

'Yes, of course,' Autumn agreed automatically. 'If you'll excuse me a moment, I'll go and tell him you're here.'

She turned to go and Pauline said quickly, 'Just a moment. I'd like to speak to you first.'

Autumn half turned so that they were looking at each other. 'Yes?'

But now Pauline seemed to be in no hurry to say whatever she had wanted to say. Instead she took in every detail of

Autumn's softly draped winter-green velvet dress, her
loosely-curled copper hair, her cool, questioning gaze.
'You're going out tonight?' she asked at last.

'Yes,' agreed Autumn briefly. Now she looked boldly at
Pauline, who was dressed in white, clinging knit. 'Are you?'

The other woman looked momentarily taken aback, but
she seemed to collect herself quickly. 'Yes, of course. I had
to go out, so I thought it would save Bill a trip by coming
by for him here since I was already so near.'

'I'm sure he'll be delighted,' said Autumn in a deadpan
voice. 'I'll just go and tell . . .'

'Please, come and sit down a moment. I'd like to get to
know you,' Pauline said with an air of great friendliness. She
smiled charmingly and added, 'Bill never speaks of you to
me, but then,' she excused his neglectfulness lightly, 'we're
always so busy talking of our two selves when we're together. You understand, I'm sure.'

'Naturally,' Autumn agreed, sizzling beneath the cool expression on the other woman's face. 'Bill never speaks to me
of you, either,' she said.

'But of course he wouldn't discuss me with you,' Pauline
purred. 'After all, you're his hired help, while I'm the
woman he intends to marry.'

If there hadn't been a timely interruption at that moment,
Autumn felt she wouldn't have been held responsible for
anything rash she might have said or done. But two things
happened at once. The doorbell rang a second time and Bill
came bounding down the stairs and across the hall. He
glanced through the open doorway and saw both women
just as Autumn was rising. He waved a hand at her and
called, 'Sit down. I'll answer the door.'

A moment later he entered the room, following Ellis.

Pauline fluttered silky dark lashes at both men, and angry
as she was, Autumn had to admire the other woman's tech-
nique. She had it down so perfectly—and so syrupy! 'My
gracious,' Pauline exclaimed, 'two handsome men at once!
Aren't we lucky?' she demanded of Autumn, never in the

least expecting an answer. 'Ellis, how is it that you've escaped marriage so far?' She gave a little smile and answered her own question with another. 'But perhaps you soon will be caught in that trap, eh?' she ended with a sly glance in Autumn's direction. Still holding stage centre, she now turned towards Bill, smiling intimately. 'Darling, I thought I'd surprise you and come by to pick you up this evening. I was already in town, so I didn't see the need for you to drive all the way out to my house.'

'That was thoughtful of you,' Bill answered in a deceptively bland voice. Autumn glanced sharply at him. Acutely attuned to his moods as she was these days, she saw that he was burningly furious about something, though he was holding it in tight rein.

'Are you ready to go?' Ellis asked Autumn now, breaking in on her conjectures about Bill's mood.

'Yes, of course. Just let me get my coat.'

Before she could leave the room, Bill asked casually, 'Where are you two going tonight?'

'The Country Club,' Ellis answered with obvious reluctance.

For just an instant Bill's eyes met and held Autumn's. 'That's where we're headed, too,' he said now to Ellis, and added smoothly, 'Why don't we make it a foursome?'

The plan met favour with nobody as far as Autumn could see. The smile on Pauline's lips vanished swiftly beneath a stormy cloud and Ellis looked anything but pleased. And as for herself, she hated it. How in the world could she manage a whole evening in Bill's company? And especially with Pauline along, vivid evidence that his love was already claimed, that her own was doomed only to concealed and permanent unhappiness.

But to her dismay, Ellis agreed to the suggestion and before she realised it they were all being shepherded out of the door and into the cold night air by Bill, who was now wearing a self-satisfied expression. As why shouldn't he, she thought bitterly. His object had been to spoil her evening

with Ellis, of course, what else? And in that he had succeeded. Of course he had also spoiled his own evening alone
with Pauline, but she supposed he must have considered it
worth the cost. Though, judging by Pauline's expression,
she had a feeling that the other girl didn't agree with him.

Somehow they got through the dinner, though Autumn
would have been hard put to it to list the menu if someone
had demanded it of her. She was too sharply aware of the
man across the table who, now that he had got his way,
seemed to have all but forgotten that another couple was
there. He devoted his attention throughout dinner almost
exclusively to the tiny raven-haired woman at his side.

As soon as they had finished dinner Ellis asked Autumn
to dance. She rose with relief, glad to be able to get away
from the constricting presence of the other couple—at least
for a brief time.

'Not quite the same as being on our own, is it?' Ellis said
as soon as they were safely away from the table.

She glanced back to see that Bill and Pauline were rising
to dance, too, and she sighed. 'No,' she agreed. 'It's not the
same at all.'

'I wonder why Robichaux wanted to team up with us?'
Ellis mused in an irritable voice. 'I mean, it's not as if he
and I are friends, and I don't think you and Pauline are,
are you?'

'Friends?' Autumn all but laughed, but she answered
politely enough, 'I'm afraid I don't know her very well.'

'So,' he pursued the subject at hand, 'I wonder why he
wanted to come along with us?'

Autumn shrugged. 'Who knows?' she said rather sharply.
She was now as glad for the music to end as she had been
for it to begin. If all Ellis wanted to do while they danced together was to discuss Bill and his possible motives for join-
ing their party tonight, then she'd rather sit at the table,
even though it *was* right beneath Bill's nose.

But she didn't sit long. The next number the band struck
up was a slow, romantic one, and Bill was suddenly at her

side, asking her to dance. Somehow she hadn't anticipated this.

His arm slid round her waist while his left hand took her right one and smoothly, like gliding on ice, they began to dance.

After a moment he said, 'We fit together perfectly.'

She knew what he meant. Their steps matched as though choreographed, and their bodies seemed to merge and blend into one as they dipped and swayed and turned. To Autumn it was all both exquisite pleasure and pain at once, pleasure at his touch, pain in knowing that, all too soon, the music would end.

His arm gently pressed her body closer to his and his hand tightened round hers. Now he held her so close she had no place to put her head except next to the warmth of his face and neck.

Bill turned his head only a fraction so that his lips were pressed against her ear. 'Are you having a good time, *chère*?' he asked in a caressingly intimate voice.

She tried to pull away from him, but his hold was too strong. She was forced to mumble into his collar, 'Bill, I ... I ...' She could get no further. He was nibbling ... definitely nibbling ... at her earlobe, and that and his soft breath that was tickling her neck was driving her crazy with desire. Her limbs suddenly felt about as sturdy as jelly and she grew panic-stricken. 'Let me go!' she exclaimed breathlessly. 'Stop it at once!'

At the urgency in her voice, his arm slackened and he drew apart from her. 'What's wrong?' he asked in the blandest of voices as he saw the outrage in her face.

'You know very well what's wrong!' she hissed.

His eyebrows lifted quizzically. 'What?'

She didn't answer him. She was in no mood for sparring with Bill, especially here, on a dance floor. Besides which, she was too busy fighting the emotions that clawed like a wildcat at her senses. It had taken every ounce of will that she possessed to tell him to relax his hold on her. Now, as his hand lay slackly and impersonally against her waist, she was contradictorily wishing that he still held her against his rock-hard chest, that his lips were still against her ear, that she could turn her head slightly until his lips met hers. And yet even still more than that did she want!

She squeezed her eyes shut for an instant, praying she could hide the aching desire in them. But when she opened them again, she met a cold, angry face. 'I didn't realise I had really offended you,' he said icily. 'For a moment there, I thought ... but I suppose Naquin holds a claim to you. Although I think you're making a big mistake there. He can never satisfy a passionate-natured woman such as you ... a dry, legal-minded person like him.'

'And ... and how do you know whether or not I've a passionate nature?' she asked through stiff lips.

His smile was mocking and he shook his head slightly. 'I merely meant that all beautiful red-haired women are supposed to be as passionate as they're tempestuous.'

Autumn felt let down at the impersonal reply and apparently he knew it and was amused by it, because as the music ended and they turned to begin weaving their way back to the table, he bent and whispered, 'Perhaps you'll let me test my theory some time?'

She half-turned and glared at him furiously. 'You know,' she said conversationally, as she knotted her hands at her side, 'sometimes I actually hate you.'

'Ah,' he mocked, 'how nice to know it's only *sometimes*.'

There was no time to frame a retort to that because by then they had reached their table and Ellis and Pauline. As Autumn sat down beside Ellis, she gave him a winning smile and made light remark and thereafter contrived to ignore Bill altogether—which actually wasn't too difficult, because for the remainder of the evening he devoted his attentions strictly to Pauline. Not once did he again ask Autumn to dance. And as for herself, she wasn't quite sure whether she was glad or sorry.

*

For the next week or so, Autumn renewed her efforts to stay out of Bill's way, and, to her chagrin, he seemed not only to be aware of it, but to also be aware of the reason behind it. It was as though he could read the breathless panic she felt whenever he stood too close to her in the office or when his hand accidentally brushed hers as she handed him a patient's chart. And whenever she allowed her wayward thoughts to stray back to the way he had held her when they danced, her heart raced.

She realised that she had to get herself in hand. She simply could not continue this way, nervous whenever Bill was around, panic-stricken if he came too close. If it got any worse, one of them would have to leave Bellefleur, and that thought was far too painful even to contemplate. She couldn't imagine Bill living anywhere else and, for herself, she had grown to adore St Pierre and Bellefleur alike, quite divorced from any feelings she had about Dr William Robichaux.

It was that determination, more than anything else, to prove to herself that she could be in close proximity to him and remain indifferent, that prompted her to accept his unexpected invitation to go fishing.

It was on a Friday night at dinner when he made the suggestion. The weather had turned unseasonably warm, more like late September than mid-November, with more warm weather predicted. 'I was glancing over the appointment book for tomorrow morning,' Bill said as he carved the roast, 'and we only have a couple of early appointments. Why don't we close shop early, say around ten-thirty, and go fishing. I heard you tell Bertha one day that you wanted to try.'

'I'd love to,' she agreed at once, though she was inwardly quaking at the thought of spending hours alone in his company. 'Will we fish from the bank?'

'No, I've got a motor boat, we'll go in that. There's a fresh water lake about ten miles away. We'll fish there.'

'Sounds great,' she responded. Then, with a grin, she said

truthfully, 'But I have to warn you, it's been years since I've been fishing. Since my dad used to take me as a child.'

'A real greenhorn?' he replied. 'That's okay. I'm willing to play instructor.'

'Who knows,' Autumn laughed as she got into the spirit of the idea, 'I might even accidentally catch something!'

'You might at that,' he agreed. 'By the way, be sure and tell Bertha we want her to pack up a picnic lunch. We can eat in the boat.'

Autumn did as she was told as soon as the meal was over and Bertha nodded agreeably as she bent over the sink, washing dishes. 'I'll pack enough for two meals, yes,' she said.

'Two? We'll only be away at noon, surely,' said Autumn.

Bertha chuckled as she scrubbed a plate. 'You've never been fishing with Dr Billy,' she stated. 'Sometime he get carried away, him, and he don't know when to come home if them fish is biting. So I'll pack enough to be on the safe side. I don't want you going hungry, no.'

'Me either,' Autumn laughed. 'I'm afraid you've built up my appetite so much with all your good Cajun cooking that nowadays I'm absolutely starving on the dot at meal times. So if you think we're likely to be late coming in, do put in some extra sandwiches or something.'

Bertha laughed and surveyed Autumn's figure with approving eyes. 'We have built you up a little bit, yes,' she said in a pleased voice. 'You're not such a skinny rail as you were when you come here.'

'I know,' Autumn sighed. 'If I ever want to go back to modelling I'll have to go on a strict diet.'

'Diet, humph!' Bertha snorted. She took a tea-towel and waved it threateningly at Autumn. 'Shoo! Just get right out of my kitchen with your silly diet talk!'

Autumn laughed and ran out, enjoying Bertha's irate tirade. She had mentioned diet to be deliberately provocative, knowing full well she would get the housekeeper riled. Bertha figured that if a person couldn't enjoy her delicious cooking to the fullest, then there really wasn't much use in living. Being slender and stylish was low on her list of priorities, as her own ample girth testified.

The following morning, at precisely ten-thirty, the last patient was ushered out of the door. Bill flipped the key in the lock behind him, then turned to Autumn, eyeing her green and white polka-dotted dress dubiously. 'You've got exactly fifteen minutes to get changed,' he told her. 'Wear your oldest beat-up clothes. That is,' he qualified, 'if you happen to *own* anything like that.'

She lifted eyebrows in mock surprise. 'But I bought a new Bill Blass just for the occasion,' she informed him jokingly. 'Just wait till you see it!' At his raised eyebrows, she turned and ran out of the room.

In her bedroom upstairs she clambered into a pair of totally disreputable faded Levis, a plaid red flannel shirt that had belonged to her father ten years previously and that now flopped around her airily, and then she tucked her vivid hair up beneath a green baseball cap with a bright yellow M on the front. She couldn't even recall where it had come from and had been surprised last night when she had dug in her trunk for the jeans and had come across it. She had supposed she had thrown it away in New York when she had been packing to come south. Now she grinned at her reflection in the mirror. Dr Robichaux could hardly accuse her of looking like a model today!

He was waiting for her on the back porch along with their fishing gear and a wicker picnic basket. He glanced up casually when the door opened, and his eyes widened. 'What every well-dressed lady is wearing this season, I presume?'

Autumn laughed. 'Exactly,' she said as she lightly touched the brim of her cap in salute.

He studied her thoughtfully, then nodded briefly. 'I can't truly call you beautiful today,' he said.

'That's fine,' she replied tartly. 'Then maybe you'll approve of my looks today for a change.'

'Oh, I approve,' he agreed swiftly. 'Instead of a beautiful

woman, today you look more like an exceedingly pretty twelve-year-old girl.'

'If that's true, then I'll behave like a twelve-year-old,' she told him, and stuck out her tongue at him.

He smiled slowly. 'Better not get too smart-aleck with your elders, my girl, or you just might get a spanking.'

'You wouldn't dare!' she said impetuously.

'Think not?' he challenged. 'Behave yourself—or you'll soon find out!'

Bayou Cache, which ran in front of Bellefleur, was too clogged with water hyacinth for any navigation. Bill drove a short distance to another bayou, where he launched his small boat with its outboard motor.

Once they got under way it was impossible to talk above the noise of the motor, but Autumn found she didn't mind that in the least. She was too interested in the scenery around her.

There was something haunting and mysterious about the dark water and the thicket of trees that lined the bayou banks. There were giant oaks that sometimes met in the middle across the water, dripping their shawls of grey Spanish moss; weeping willows bowed low over the muddy banks; tangled vines crept up tree trunks and fans of vivid green palmettos ran rampant along the shores.

As long as they travelled the bayou, Autumn could see an occasional house and later, as they wound further from civilisation, a crudely constructed cabin or two that were used by fishermen or trappers.

They reached the swamps and left the open bayou. Now vegetation seemed to crowd round them. Everywhere were tiny islands with bore trees and palmettos. Cypress trees thrust tall trunks and numerous knees up through the murky waters. Moss hung so low from branches that Autumn could reach out her hand and touch it.

A few minutes later, after weaving round the small bodies of land in a seemingly senseless fashion, they reached a more open area and headed straight towards the centre.

There Bill cut the motor at last.

It was a silent world and the quiet almost seemed to press down upon them like weights, broken only by the call of a distant bird. It was all eerily beautiful and even a bit frightening, and Autumn knew she only felt safe because of the man sitting opposite her.

He looked up suddenly and smiled at her. Instantly, the gloomy, forbidding atmosphere which had hung so heavy was dispelled as though by a puff of magic, and the day was bright with sunshine again. Autumn smiled back.

'Well,' he asked, 'and what do you think of it?'

'It's beautiful,' she admitted, 'but rather frightening, too,' she added truthfully. 'It's so remote from anything I've ever seen before.'

He nodded. 'Louisiana swamps are an experience to someone who sees them for the first time.'

'I'll say,' she agreed. 'Are there any alligators here?' she asked as she glanced around rather apprehensively. She had only at that moment dredged up from her subconscious some long-forgotten fragment of information she had read somewhere concerning the inhabitants of swamp areas.

'Not too many around here,' he answered, 'though south Louisiana is known for them, all right. But this particular spot, they're not too plentiful.'

'Good,' she said with visible relief.

'We have our share of water moccasins, however,' he informed her quite cheerfully.

'You just *had* to say that, didn't you?' She made a face at him and shuddered. 'I certainly hope we don't meet up with any.'

Bill laughed, handed her a rod and enquired whether she knew how to cast. At her affirmative nod, he reached for his own rod. 'Need to fish deep,' he advised. 'Even though the weather's been mild lately, the bass know it's almost winter.'

Autumn couldn't remember when she had last enjoyed a day so much. The afternoon wore itself away lazily while the stringer that dangled from the side of the boat into the water boasted a gradually growing number of bass and the enormous pile of food in the picnic hamper dwindled as the two people nibbled and fished, but rarely spoke.

It was an incredibly peaceful silence—a companionable quiet that soothed Autumn and made her almost wish that the day would never have to end.

By late afternoon, however, they began to be glad of the jackets they had brought along. A suddenly sprung up wind whistled through the trees around them and Bill eyed the sky frowningly. 'We're in for some rain soon,' he told her, 'or I miss my guess.'

'Will we have time to make it back home before it starts?' she asked anxiously as she, too, studied the now overcast grey sky. She didn't relish the idea of being caught in a boat during a rainstorm.

'I think so,' he said reassuringly. 'We'll head in now.' He busied himself stowing rods beneath the seats, then pulling the stringer of bass in, so that the fish flopped haphazardly at Autumn's feet, shaking droplets of water on to her legs.

Bill started the motor and they were off, weaving slowly once more between the tall cypresses which cast weird shadows across the water. It seemed to Autumn that the sky grew markedly darker and the air distinctly more chilly with every passing moment.

It was just as the first few rain drops fell upon her hair that Autumn made her dismaying discovery. She had glanced idly down into the bottom of the boat, aware that her feet felt a bit colder and wetter than before. And no wonder! The bottom was covered with an alarming amount of water.

Her mouth was cottony with fear as she called out, 'B-B-Bill!'

He had been gazing out over the water, watching his course between the swampy islands, but at the sound of her voice, he turned round quickly.

'What's the matter?' he asked sharply. 'Are you hurt?'

'N-no.' She shook her head. 'I ... I'm fine. It ... It's ... look!' She pointed towards her feet.

'My God!' he muttered beneath his breath as he stared incredulously at the water which even now was licking at the soles of his shoes. 'We've sprung a leak!'

'H-how could it have happened?' she asked hoarsely.

Bill thrust long fingers agitatedly through his thick hair, so that a dark lock flopped over his forehead. 'We must have gone over a tree that was hidden just beneath the surface,' he mused as he stared at the creeping level of water around their feet.

His head came up and his eyes met hers, and just at that moment the rain began. It was icy cold and, as the wind picked up behind them from the north, Autumn's teeth chattered as she tried to hunch further down into her jacket.

'We'll have to make for a fisherman's cabin I know of,' Bill decided. 'It's roughly about a mile from here.'

'Do you ... do you think we can make it?' Autumn asked anxiously as she warily eyed the water which was inching up around her ankles.

'We must,' Bill said quietly. He picked up an empty soft drink can and handed it to her. 'While I guide the boat, you start bailing,' he ordered. 'This won't help much, but it won't hurt either.'

She knew better than to ask it, but even so the words just popped out, unbidden. 'Is there any chance at all of making it home?'

'You mean tonight?'

She nodded and he answered curtly, 'Not a chance. Unless,' he qualified, 'you plan to swim. Why? Do you have a date with Naquin tonight?' The words came out hard and cold.

'As a matter of fact, I do,' she answered, equally coldly. What right did he have of being rude to her just because she might have plans for the evening?

'Then he won't like this at all, will he?' he commented.

'Your spending the night with me alone out in the middle of the swamps?'

'I don't much like it myself,' she snapped angrily.

For a moment he was silent, then he smiled and said evenly, 'Maybe I'll change your mind. After all, I'll have the whole night in which to do it.'

CHAPTER EIGHT

AFTER Bill's threatening, taunting words, at first Autumn was too incensed even to frame a suitable retort and then the rain had come even harder. Bill had given his entire attention to navigating the crippled boat through the swamps to a place of safety and Autumn had been too busy bailing water and being frightened to think of continuing the argument. The trees and swamps which had seemed gloomily mysterious earlier in the light of day now were threatening and treacherous. Autumn knew that some of the land masses that looked so solid were actually quicksand and that a human could be swallowed up by it in a matter of minutes. She shuddered at the thought. Here they were, moving slowly in a leaking boat across water that could be concealing alligators and water moccasins, between tiny islands that could be quicksand. And despite her anger, she knew that if she were with anyone else except Bill Robichaux, she would be a gibbering idiot by now from the terror. But Bill kept his cool. He nosed the boat forward for a time and when he saw that she was losing her battle at bailing, he stopped to help until the water level was low enough to continue again.

It grew swiftly dark, and dark out here in the swamps was a total darkness such as Autumn had never before experienced. The rain came harder so that they were both soaked thoroughly. Autumn hunched over, her hands like icicles as she filled the soft drink can with water, emptied it overboard, then repeated the process. She felt frozen and stiff all over from the cold and the wet, but she didn't dare stop her chore for so much as an instant. She was sure that, if she ever did, the cold would finish its work and leave her so rigid that she couldn't possibly move again. She looked

115

at Bill, and knew it must be the same for him. His face and hands were being battered by both the icy rain and the spray of water that flew up from the swamp.

Just when she thought she couldn't continue one more instant, the bow touched shore. Bill cut the motor and jumped out with the rope so that he could secure the boat to a piling. Autumn sat back and looked up. It was so dark that she could only just barely see the outline of a cabin among the dark shadows of bearded cypress trees.

Bill had finished knotting the rope to the piling and now he waded back into the water. 'Give me your hand,' he told her. 'I'll help you out.'

She held out a cold hand awkwardly and placed it into his. Even though they were both soaking wet and cold, somehow his clasp seemed warm. As she brought the other hand up and placed it on his shoulder to steady herself as she jumped out, her face was so close to his that she could actually feel his breath on her cheek. She was glad of the shielding darkness so that he couldn't see how suddenly flustered she felt.

Once her feet were on solid ground, she quickly removed her hand from his shoulder and tugged her other hand free from his. He released it with unflattering speed and reached back into the boat. 'Here,' he mumbled over his shoulder. 'Can you carry the picnic basket? And the flashlight?' He dug around in one of the boat seats' storage compartments and suddenly a light sprang to life in the coffee-thick darkness.

He handed Autumn both the basket and the flashlight and ordered, 'Hold the light for me. I'm going to get the ice chest.' After he had it over the side of the boat, he turned towards her. 'You'll have to lead the way,' he said. 'Shine the light on the ground and walk carefully. The ground is uneven.'

Slowly they made their way the few yards from the water's edge to the cabin, which Autumn was surprised to discover was on stilts. She had to mount steps up to a narrow porch, turning after each step and flashing the light down so Bill could see his way.

'Go ahead and open the door,' he told her. 'It isn't locked.'

When he reached the porch, she entered, flashing the light ahead. The light picked out a kitchen table and she headed towards it and put down the burden of the picnic basket. She cast the glow back towards Bill and found that he had placed the ice chest on the floor next to the door.

He came across the room and went to a cupboard against the wall. Unerringly, he located a lantern which he carried over to the table. As he bent over the lantern with a box of matches in his hands, he requested, 'Hold the flashlight over my shoulder, will you?'

She moved to stand just behind him and held the light steady. A moment later the entire room lighted up and for the first time she took stock of her surroundings.

It was a one-room cabin, finished off very roughly. Supporting two-by-fours that held up the walls had not been covered over. Instead, they doubled as shelves and Autumn saw they contained various items such as paperback novels, bandages and drug store antibiotic sprays and ointments, a snakebite kit, a couple of empty soft drink bottles with candles stuck into their mouths and a flashlight. Along one wall was a double bed, its mattress covered with protective plastic. At its foot was a long metal chest. Along the opposite wall was a kitchen work counter beneath the only window. Beside it was a very old gas stove. In the centre of the room was a wooden table with three mismatched chairs around it. That completed the furnishings.

Bill grabbed up the flashlight and headed back to the door. 'I'm going outside to turn on the butane for the stove,' he said. Then he pointed towards the metal chest at the foot of the bed. 'That should contain some sheets and pillows and blankets. Better get out of those wet clothes and wrap up in one of the blankets—I'll stay outside until you're respectable,' he added, a glint of mockery in his eyes. As he

saw that she was about to protest, the hint of amusement
vanished and he said harshly, 'Now don't argue. You can't
possibly remain in those wet clothes all night.'

As he turned away and went through the door, Autumn
let him go without a word. She could hardly explain to him
that her objection hadn't been about getting out of the wet
clothes, but about his leaving her here alone. Right now
a bigger terror than having him in the same room while she
undressed was having him outside in that rain-flooded
swamp among unknown horrors. What if he got lost or hurt
out there? What would she do in this place all alone? She
closed her eyes and knotted her hands at her sides, sternly
suppressing the wild impulse she had to fling open the
door and run after him.

After a moment, with stilted, cold fingers, she began re-
moving her dripping clothes.

Inside the metal chest she discovered not only the sheets,
pillows and blankets but also a large supply of safety pins,
a woman's hair net, a man's shirt and a pair of trousers, one
child's sock and three bath towels. She seized up one of
the towels and vigorously began to rub herself dry.

The rubbing brought a warm red glow to her skin, but it
was still freezing cold in the room, so she hurriedly wrapped
herself inside one of the blankets, casting long and regretful
glances at the man's pants and shirt. With a sigh, she took
the safety pin and draped the blanket in such a way that
she could wear it and move, too, without any danger of its
falling off. One long corner of soft blue wool hugged across
her left shoulder before it came to rest with a secure pin
just above her right breast. Others pins served as buttons
down the sides. Of course her new designer's creation was a
bit too long and dragged the floor, but what matter? At
least she was dry and covered up and a lot warmer by far
than she had been.

Finally she was satisfied. Then she reached back into the
chest and pulled out the man's clothing and another towel,
all of which she draped over the back of a chair. Then she

crossed the room and opened the door.

'Bill!' she called out, trying to peer through the blinding rain. 'Bill, I'm dressed. You can come back inside now.'

Only the rain hissing against the tin roof answered her. After a moment she called again and there was a rising inflection of panic in her voice. She strained her eyes as she peered out through the driving rain into the shrouding darkness. 'Bill! Bill!'

She turned back into the room, glancing around wildly. It seemed like a friendly prison, this dimly-lit room. She wondered if she should pull back on her wet clothes and go out to search for him. But where to start? She didn't know this swampy island with its cypresses and palmettos at all. She was sure to get lost in no time outside in the darkness in these untame, strange surroundings. Yet she couldn't *not* go. Suppose Bill were lying injured somewhere?

She reached out a hand for her wet, crumpled Levis. Behind her came a shuffling noise at the door, and she whirled, her eyes wide, dark pools of fear. A stifled cry sounded through her parted lips. She wasn't even aware of the tears that were coursing down her cheeks. She was only aware of the man in the doorway and of how wildly glad she was to see him.

'Bill!' she cried out as she rushed to him and flung herself into his arms. 'Oh, Bill!'

His two hands gripped her arms and held her a little away from him. 'You thought I'd gone away and left you?' he demanded incredulously.

'No! No!' she sobbed out. 'You don't understand. I thought you were lost ... or hurt ... or ...' she choked, 'even dead!'

He raised his eyebrows and laughed. 'You silly little goose,' he said. 'I wasn't gone *that* long.'

'But I called and called and you didn't answer,' she managed to get out, even as she was struggling to get control of herself.

'I went back down to the boat to secure it better for the

night and then I brought the stringer of fish back. They're on the porch—I thought we might as well cook them for our supper. I suppose with it raining so hard I couldn't hear you call while I was down at the water's edge. Are you going to be all right now?'

She nodded, staring at the floor, so ashamed now at her silly emotional outburst that she was embarrassed to look at him.

'You look very lovely in that ... whatever kind of outfit you can call it,' he said unexpectedly, 'but I'm getting you all drenched.'

She looked at him quickly, still suspicious when he paid her compliments, but his expression was matter-of-fact. Then, 'My goodness, you'll freeze to death if you don't get out of those wet clothes,' she said. 'I found a shirt and a pair of pants in the chest that I suppose you can wear. You'd better change at once.'

He shook his head. 'Not just yet. I'm going to light the stove so the room will start warming up and then I'm going back out on the porch to clean the fish. No sense changing before that's done.'

He lit the stove as Autumn stood by and watched, then he pointed to the cupboards. 'There's usually some cooking oil and cornmeal in there. And maybe a can of beans or something. Why don't you dig and see what you can find for our supper?'

She nodded and as he went back outside, obediently began her search. Relief that Bill was indeed safe and unharmed had left her limp for a time, but now that she was more her normal self, she realised suddenly that she was absolutely starved, and surely if she were, Bill must be even more so after all his efforts.

By the time he had the bass cleaned and brought them inside, Autumn had accomplished a great deal. The stove had heated the room beautifully and, in the meantime, she had discovered a can of coffee and a coffee pot. She took some of the ice from the ice chest and boiled it to make the coffee. Then she discovered a skillet, the cooking oil and cornmeal for the fish and also a can of green beans. Left over from all the food Bertha had packed this morning were a few boiled eggs, a couple of apples, a large bag of potato chips, some bread rolls, a few slices of ham and half a pecan pie. Autumn studied the loot and decided the eggs, ham and bread would be reserved for breakfast. The remainder would do for tonight.

'Do I smell coffee?' Bill asked as he came in on a breath of frosty air and deposited the fish on the counter.

'Scalding hot coffee,' she assured him. 'While you change into those dry clothes, I'll pour you a cup.'

'I'd appreciate that,' he said and, as she looked at him, for the first time she realised just how tired he must be. There was a blue, pinched look about his mouth that she didn't like at all. He had been cold and wet far too long.

She took two coffee mugs down from hooks on the wall and filled them with the steaming, strong coffee. Then she poured oil into the skillet, placed it on a burner to heat and began seasoning the fish.

Bill joined her and picked up one of the mugs of coffee and took a deep swallow.

'Better?' she asked as their eyes met over the coffee mug.

'Not bad for a model,' he said mischievously, then glanced down at his ill-fitting clothes. 'We're a team, aren't we? Suppose we could set a new fashion in New York if we modelled these outfits?'

Autumn laughed. 'Don't knock them,' she told him. 'At least they're better than what we were wearing. We're dry now. And it's warmed up a lot in here since you lit the stove. Are you thawing any yourself?' she asked anxiously as he gulped more of the scalding coffee and held his mug out for her to fill again.

'I'm beginning to,' he acknowledged. 'I don't mind telling you I was beginning to feel pretty frostbitten.'

'You'll be lucky if you don't come down with pneumonia,' she said worriedly.

'Dr McBride speaking?' he laughed. When her face burned a deep shade of pink, he said, 'What about you? You were just as wet as me.'

'But not for as long,' she said swiftly.

There was a short silence and then he said, 'You know, I get the feeling that you actually are concerned about me.'

'Of course I'm concerned about you!' she answered indignantly.

'Why?' The one word was said in a quiet voice, but it exploded over Autumn like the noise and violence of a rocket.

'W-why?' she stammered, parrot-fashion. She couldn't speak the truth, of course. That she was concerned mostly because she loved him. That she would *always* be concerned about his health and well-being as long as she lived. No, she couldn't speak a word of truth about what was in her secret heart. 'Why, because I would care about anyone under the same circumstances,' she said at last.

'And would you fling yourself into just anyone's arms if you found they weren't missing or lost after all?'

Her face burned now and her lower lip trembled. She turned away from him quickly. 'I ... I'm sorry about that,' she choked out. 'I ... I ...'

He touched her arm and she slowly turned her head once again. 'Don't be sorry,' he said, and there was another of those gleams of humour in his eyes. 'You can do it again if you like.'

Now she stuck her tongue out at him saucily. 'Well, I only did it because ...'

He held up a hand to stop the flow of words. 'I know,' he said patiently. 'Only because you were scared and under the circumstances it really didn't matter who it was. All right, I won't go getting a swelled head if that's what's bothering you. Now,' he added in an entirely different tone of voice, 'if you'll move out of the way, I'll fry that fish.'

She stood her ground and shook her head. 'No, you won't,' she told him firmly. 'You had to clean it. Sit down now and rest while you warm up. I'll cook the supper.'

'Very domestic,' he commented. 'We could be an old married couple.'

'Only we aren't,' she pointed out tartly. 'Now move out of my way.'

The meal was delicious despite the unnerving circumstances, and afterwards, in order to wash up the dishes, Autumn boiled up some old water she had found stored beneath the counter in plastic milk jugs.

She washed and Bill dried, and as she stored away the skillet beneath the counter, he went across to the door and stepped outside on to the porch.

A minute or so later he came back inside. 'Whew!' he exclaimed as he quickly shut the door against the frigid air. 'Would you believe it's actually *sleeting* out there? I picked a hell of a day to take you fishing, didn't I?'

'Well, it was warm and sunny when we started out,' she told him reasonably. 'How could you know the weather would turn so horrible or that the boat would leak?'

He shrugged. 'With all this rain and wind, not to mention ice and darkness, I don't imagine a good search will get under way until tomorrow at daylight,' he told her frankly.

She nodded, having her own private opinion confirmed. 'And the chances of their looking for us here at this particular cabin?'

'There's the trouble,' he said. 'This is Les LeCompte's fishing camp. Once in a while I spend a night up here, but whether he'll think to send the searchers to check here or not, I just can't say. They'll be out looking for us on the lake first.'

'In other words,' she said, 'we might be rescued tomorrow, but then again . . .'

He nodded and put it into words. 'But then again it may be days.'

She thought about that for a long moment, then she said briskly, 'Well, I hope to goodness we can catch enough fish in the middle of this southern version of the North Pole blizzard to keep us in food.'

Unexpectedly, he threw back his head and laughed. 'You *are* a most unusual girl, Autumn. For all your exotic beauty, you're very practical.'

But Autumn was not feeling very practical as the minutes pushed their way towards bedtime. As the two of them sat near the stove to keep warm, with their wet clothes dangling from the third chair, the table and the counter in the hopes of drying them quickly, Autumn assessed the situation thoroughly. First, there was only one bed; second, the butane supply was not inexhaustible. It would have to be conserved because they might actually be here for days. Secondly, people died every year in hunting cabins such as this from leaving the gas on overnight. Thirdly, once the stove was off, the room would quickly grow extremely cold, and fourthly, there were only two blankets, one of which she was now wearing. And one blanket would not ward off the cold for the entire night very well. But if she took off the blanket in order to share both blankets and the bed with Bill, she would have to sleep clad only in her now drying undies. The only alternative was to keep the blanket on, let him wrap up in the other, and one of them sleep on the bed while the other one slept on the chairs or the floor, both of which were unadorned wood and uncompromisingly hard.

He glanced over at her with a derisive expression on his face. 'I'm not going to sleep on the floor or chairs when there's a perfectly good bed with room enough for the both of us.'

She all but jumped out of her chair, so startled was she at his words. 'How . . . how did you know . . .?' she began.

He shrugged. 'You have a very expressive face.'

'A model certainly isn't supposed to.'

'Maybe you do because you're no longer a model?'

It was her turn to shrug. 'I suppose,' she agreed dully. Her face heated as she thought of the main subject at hand. And this thing *had* to be hashed out, regardless of how distasteful it seemed. And she had not entirely forgotten Bill's earlier taunt in the boat despite his easy-going, prosaic behaviour since. He had said he might make her *like* being alone with him and that he'd have the whole night to do it. There had been no mistaking his meaning.

Again, he seemed to read her mind. 'I'd never want a woman I had to *force*,' he said, bringing a new flood of embarrassment over her. 'I like my women soft and willing, and right now you look about as soft as a wooden Indian. About as ferocious, too.' He stood up. 'I'm going to make the bed now. You can do as you damn please for the night, but if I'm allowed to make a suggestion, your best bet would be to get back into those things——' He waved a hand in the direction of her bra and panties which were draped like bold banners over the back of a chair '—which look dry enough, and put this shirt on over them and come to bed with me where we can both be warm.' He unbuttoned the too large shirt he'd been wearing and flung it at her, leaving his broad chest bare before he reached into the metal chest and pulled out a bed sheet.

Autumn sat rooted to her chair for a long moment. Indecision whirled through her brain. But then she suddenly made her decision and stood up, still clutching the shirt Bill had thrown at her. His bronze-coloured back was turned to her as he bent over the bed, smoothing out the white sheet. 'If ... if you'll not turn around for a few minutes, I'll be grateful,' she said.

'Yours to obey,' he replied easily.

With nervous hands she unpinned the blanket and let it slide to the floor. Hurriedly she scrambled into the thin wisps of underwear, wishing fervently that they were a bit more substantial, then she slipped into the flannel shirt that still retained some of the heat from Bill's chest. After that, there was nothing more to do except move self-consciously around to the opposite side of the bed and help him finish preparing it.

Ten minutes later Autumn was beneath the blankets and Bill switched off both stove and lantern. A moment later, the other side of the bed sagged beneath his weight as he sat down on it. Then he stretched out full length and pulled the blankets up over his body.

Autumn huddled far to the edge of her side of the bed, almost scarcely daring to breathe. 'Sweet dreams,' he said.

'G-goodnight,' she answered stiffly.

The bed moved and she froze, but a moment later, chagrined, she realised Bill had merely turned over so that he was facing away from her. And minutes later his rhythmic breathing told her he was already asleep. So much for his intentions, she thought, and laughed quietly at herself and her absurd fears. She should have known that he would never take advantage of a situation like this and force his attentions upon her.

But now that he was asleep she could lower her guard and go back and relive that moment when she had thought he was lost or injured and she had flung herself into his arms, and then she was asleep herself, from a combination of exhaustion, delicious warmth and the lulling sound of rain mixed with sleet falling against the tin roof.

Once she awoke and realised that something was different. For a minute she couldn't think what it might be, but then suddenly she knew. Bill had turned over during the night and now his chest was pressed next to her back, his left arm was draped casually across her waist and his face was warm against her neck. She lay still for a long moment, wondering what she should do. It felt so cosily wonderful, the warmth of his body so close to hers. She closed her eyes and savoured the sensation, just for a moment—and allowed her mind to dwell upon how it would feel to lie in his arms this way every night after an evening of lovemaking.

Her face grew hot at her imaginings. She was really going to have to get hold of herself and her love for Bill before it caused her to do something foolish, like turn over so that her face would be next to his, as she yearned to do. Instead, she forced herself to try to withdraw from his arm.

But at her slight movement, his hand pressed against her waist, locking her body into place beside him, and his face actually nuzzled against her neck. 'Ummm,' he mumbled in his sleep. 'So sweet, *chère*. So sweet.'

She stiffened, positive that he could not mean her in his dream. He must be dreaming of Pauline. She tried once more to withdraw gently from his embrace, but he merely pressed her body closer to his again and gave a great sigh. Finally she relaxed against him. It was bittersweet, this experience, but she would get what enjoyment she could from it because this situation was not likely ever to be repeated once they were rescued from their little island. And that could be any time.

So with a great sigh of her own she closed her eyes and drifted off to sleep again, this time blissfully unconcerned about the propriety of the arrangement.

CHAPTER NINE

'RISE and shine, *chère*!' Autumn opened her eyes to find Bill towering over her as he stood next to the bed. 'I've brought your coffee,' he told her.

She sat up, at once taking in her surroundings. 'The storm?' she enquired as Bill handed her the mug of steaming coffee.

'It's over,' he told her as he recrossed the room to the table where he picked up his own mug. 'It's cold as the dickens outside, but at least the sun is shining.'

She noticed now that he was dressed in the clothes and jacket he had worn yesterday and felt thankful to know their clothes had dried. 'Have you been down to check the boat?' she asked.

He nodded. 'It's a bad hole,' he told her. 'I don't know whether I can find anything to plug it up well enough to get us home.'

She studied him soberly for a long, thoughtful moment before asking, 'So we're still stuck here until we're rescued?'

He nodded again and his dark, serious eyes met hers. 'It looks that way,' he said slowly.

'All right,' she said briskly. 'Then that calls for a conference of ways and means. But first, scram so I can get dressed, will you?'

For the first time, he grinned. With his dark stubble of unshaven beard, he looked like one of Lafitte's pirates again. 'You can say that to a man you slept with all ...?'

'Doctor Robichaux!' she cut in dangerously through clenched teeth. She held the mug of coffee in a threatening position, like a baseball pitcher with a ball.

He got up from the table and moved to the door. 'All right, Miss McBride, I'll go on my rounds.'

Autumn grinned to herself in satisfaction as the door closed behind him and she uncoiled bare legs and slid out of the warm bed on to the cold floor.

Even though the stove was going, the room was still chilled from the early morning frost and Autumn lost no time at all in getting into her hopelessly wrinkled but blessedly dry Levis and flannel shirt. The tennis shoes still felt a bit damp, but that couldn't be helped. Then she ran her fingers through her tangled mass of auburn curls. She must look a real mess, with her hair dangling round her shoulders and no way to comb it into any semblance of order. The cap she had started out with the day before had blown away during the gale of a storm. Ruefully, she told herself that next time she went on a day's fishing expedition she would go fortified with little extras like toothbrush, a comb and a change of clothes, not to mention a raincoat and thermal underwear.

She found Bill down by the water's edge where he had managed to pull the boat on to the shore. 'It's a hole the size of a saucer!' he told her. 'I don't see how we could have not realised it when it happened!'

Autumn peered into the boat and saw for herself. Actually it was a jagged opening more like the rim of a half moon, but plenty large enough to be completely unseaworthy, as they had found from experience last night.'

'No sense in letting it get us down,' she told him calmly. 'What's done is done. Now I have something really serious to discuss with you,' she told him, just as though the problem with the boat was totally insignificant.

His eyes narrowed as he turned his brooding gaze on her. 'What is it?'

'Our food supply,' she said promptly. 'Thank God Bertha saw fit to pack enough food for two meals in case we were late getting home yesterday, so we've got enough left over now for one good meal. But only one good meal. Also, our water supply . . .'

'Is dwindling,' he said, nodding. 'I know. That's why I

only made enough coffee for us to each have one cup. When the water in the ice chest is gone, that's it. And it's none too clean itself, since we had cans of drinks in there on ice yesterday. But it's all we have. That water in jugs under the counter is old ... Les just leaves it up here for use in washing. What do you want to do about the food ... eat it now or wait until noon or tonight? I'm going to try to fish from the bank here, but truly, I don't think I'll have much luck. The weather's too cold and the water here isn't very deep. But we'll eat whenever you want.'

'Then I vote for around eleven,' she said promptly. 'That way it can be a late breakfast and an early lunch. But supper is a long time to have to wait. I say tomorrow's soon enough for going completely hungry, supposing we don't catch any fish.'

'Agreed,' he said. 'Now, do you want to fish with me?'

'You bet,' she told him. 'I'm going to just *will* those fish to bite my hook. We *need* that food!'

Bill grinned sympathetically as he reached for the rods. 'Good girl!'

But by the time they stopped to eat around noon, neither of them had had so much as an encouraging nibble. Autumn was conscious, as they ate, that this might be their last meal for some time. They each drank a half cup of water with the meal.

When they were finished, Bill stood up, about to go back out to fish again. As Autumn stood, too, ready to clear things away, their eyes met, and there was a flicker of humour in his eyes. 'I'll try to see this doesn't happen again,' he said.

'I wasn't aware that it was your fault,' she said. 'Unless you knocked a hole into the boat for the sheer joy of it and you suddenly developed the power to produce storms.'

He looked at her for a long, long moment and the atmosphere was charged with an electrical current. Finally he spoke. 'When we get out of this,' he said quietly, 'there's something I want to say to you.'

Autumn's heart pounded wildly all of a sudden. She gripped the back of the chair until her knuckles whitened. 'Can't you say it now?' she asked as she looked back at him steadily.

He shook his head and the spell was broken. 'No. No, I can't. This is neither the time nor the place.' He paused, then added, 'Well, back to work. It's funny, but until today I never thought of fishing as work.'

She forced herself to smile at his words before he turned to leave the room. But her heart was crying out to know what it was he wanted to say to her that couldn't be said now. Somehow she instinctively felt that, whatever it was, it was too serious, too important to be left to the vague, chancy time of 'later'. As she watched him go, depression settled upon her like a mantle. She was imagining things if she thought he meant he had something of a personal, intimate nature to say to her. That was merely wishful thinking, born of her longing for him, and she was suddenly tired ... tired of caring, tired of hoping, tired of this miserable fishing camp and the anxiety of not knowing when they would be found. Hot tears scalded her eyes and then she was just plain tired of herself as well as everything else. Angrily she brushed the tears away and set to work cleaning the cabin. She would *not* feel sorry for herself for *any* reason!

Two hours later as the two of them stood on the bank, grimly casting their fishing lines into the frigid water yet once more, they both heard the sound at the same moment. Autumn jerked her head round to look at Bill. He was looking at her, too, with a quizzical expression in his eyes. 'It's a boat!'

They both dropped their rods, cupped their hands to their lips like megaphones and started yelling. A few minutes later a boat came nosing round a bend and into view.

As it came close to shore, one of the men threw out a rope to Bill, who caught it and began securing it to the piling. The two men on the boat jumped over the sides and ran towards them.

Autumn was caught tight in a pair of arms. 'Sweetheart! I've been worried half out of my mind over you!' Ellis exclaimed. Then, before she could even catch her breath, she was being soundly kissed in full view of the other two men.

When Ellis finally released her, Autumn backed off, self-consciously dreading to have to face Bill. But she could hardly go on staring intently at the muddy ground for ever.

She lifted a delicately pink-tinted face and looked defiantly across at him. His dark eyes were stormy in his scowling face. For some reason she sensed that he actively disliked Ellis and that was all there was to it, although she would have thought that, since Ellis was one of their rescuers, Bill would be feeling a bit more in charity with him.

The other man who had come was Addie Ledet, who was looking at Autumn, and then at Bill, with an odd smile on his face, as though he was secretly amused about something. 'Well now,' Addie said heartily, 'you both look to me to be in pretty good shape after a night out in a storm. What happened?'

Bill showed him the boat and Ellis also walked over to have a look. Autumn lagged a little behind, still flustered and confused over Ellis's unexpected greeting—and Bill's obvious disapproval. She wished it hadn't happened. She wished she could explain to Bill that it didn't mean a thing to her, but of course she couldn't.

'How did you come to look for us here?' Bill asked Addie.

'Les's motor is out of commission, so he couldn't bring his boat out to look. He's riding in someone else's boat and they were going over to a different lake. But since I was coming out here, he told me to check his camp, that sometimes you spent a night or so up here. Said there was an outside chance that when the weather got bad you were able to make it here for shelter if you were in this vicinity.'

'Good old Les,' said Bill. 'And you too, Addie. Will I ever be glad to get away from this place!'

Ellis had been glancing around as the other two talked

and now his eyes widened as they came to rest on Bill. 'You mean you two spent the night together . . . inside that cabin . . . alone?' His implication was perfectly clear and Autumn felt her face scald hotly.

Bill's voice was deceptively cool. 'I think you'd better explain your meaning, Naquin,' he said.

'You know exactly what I mean,' Ellis retorted belligerently. 'If you laid so much as a finger on Autumn, I'll . . .'

'You'll what?' said Bill.

'Stop it, both of you!' Autumn exclaimed, stepping quickly between them. Her heart was thudding as she held up both hands intended to make the two men keep their distance.

'What happened in there last night, Autumn?' Ellis demanded.

Now Autumn was blazingly angry herself. She turned on Ellis with the fury of a hurricane. 'Who do you think you are, demanding answers of me?' she hissed at him. 'Whatever happened or didn't happen here last night is between Bill and me and absolutely none of your darned business!'

'You don't mean that!' Ellis exclaimed hoarsely.

'I most certainly do!' she cried. 'Now, leave me alone. I'm tired and I want to go home.'

Addie Ledet soon had them aboard his boat. Autumn sat stonily looking out over the murky swamp. Ellis sat silently beside her, while Bill sat across from them, next to Addie. He would come back another time to retrieve his boat and haul it in for repairs.

The air was sharply chilling as the boat manoeuvred its way purposefully through the shadowy swamps, beneath cypress branches overhanging with moss, around cypress knees that thrust up out of the water, brushing by thickets of palmettos and other wild vegetation.

'Autumn,' Ellis said urgently in her ear, trying to make himself heard to her above the engine, but low enough for the other men not to hear, 'I'm sorry. I lost my head, I guess, but I've been so worried about you. And then to find you'd been snug all the time alone in a cabin with Robichaux, well ...' He trailed off unhappily as it occurred to him he had once again said the wrong thing when Autumn turned to glare at him coldly. After that, they both remained in silence for the rest of the trip.

When they reached the boat launch at last, there was a small knot of people milling about. Autumn spotted Bertha among them, as well as Pauline Blanchard and Marianne Ledet.

Autumn was helped out of the boat and enveloped in Bertha's waiting arms. 'You look half frozen,' she scolded gently. 'But never mind, *chère*, we'll soon have you home and into a hot bath, yes.' Then she released her to Marianne's care while she went forward to hug her dear Dr Billy.

Autumn turned to look back and saw that as Bertha moved away from Bill, Pauline went to him and threw her arms around his neck. 'Oh, darling,' she cried out, 'I've been so terrified for you!'

At that moment Ellis reached Autumn's side and slid an arm round her waist. She saw Bill glance across as he draped an arm around Pauline's shoulders before moving away towards her waiting car.

Autumn's heart sank to zero. Impatiently she shook away Ellis's arm. 'I want you,' she said to him levelly, 'to leave me alone!'

A week later all the excitement had pretty much died down. Except for the hole still in the bottom of the boat, which had by this time been retrieved, there was no other physical evidence of the ill-fated trip or of the night Autumn and Bill had spent alone together. Even Bertha's gloomy prognostications of their getting bad colds had not come to pass. Neither Autumn nor Bill had even so much as sneezed after their ordeal. Hot baths, hot meals and a little rest had restored them both in no time.

Outside of office hours, Autumn had rarely seen Bill since their return. She assumed he was spending most of his free time with Pauline. And why not? He was probably having as big a time convincing her that his night alone with Autumn had been innocent as she would have had with Ellis, if she had cared enough to bother.

She had finally got over her anger with Ellis, and had accepted his apology. She could scarcely be so unforgiving as to continue to refuse when he had sent flowers every day and had come by the house personally every evening. But even though she considered them to be friends again, the incident had only served to give her further proof, if she needed it, that she could never love him or be his wife. She believed that a person had a right to expect complete trust from a husband or wife. And Ellis had proved that, in unusual circumstances, he instantly believed the worst.

The weather had warmed up again, beautiful and sunny and giving absolutely no hint at all that only a week ago it had been icy cold. 'I hope,' said Autumn one morning as she sat down at the kitchen table for breakfast, 'that the weather stays like this for Thanksgiving.'

'You never can tell,' Bertha said as she placed a stack of pancakes before her. 'Sometime it's warm, sometime it's cool, or rainy. But cold like last week, no. That was real odd for this early in the year. Now, speaking of Thanksgiving, what size turkey you want me to order at the butcher's?'

'I'm not sure,' said Autumn as Bill came in and sat down opposite her. As Bertha gave him a stack of pancakes and he began dousing them with thick syrup, Autumn said, 'I'm considering having a large dinner for Thanksgiving. I was thinking of inviting the Farlands, Ledets, LeComptes, Ellis and his father. What do you think, Bill?'

'Sounds fine to me,' he told her. 'But would it be too much trouble for you to invite one extra guest? Pauline?'

'Of course not,' she assured him quickly. 'Naturally you

would want her included. I'm sorry I didn't think of it myself.'

He gave her a quick look, but made no comment. She wondered what she had said to cause that look, but she didn't ask. Instead she spoke to Bertha. 'We'll work out our menu later, after I've invited everyone.'

The only refusals were Dianne and Gary Farland, who would be spending the holiday with her family in New Orleans. Autumn decided also to invite Grace Hebert, the widowed schoolteacher, to make up an even number of guests. Grace was also more in the elder Mr Naquin's age bracket, so Autumn hoped they would like each other.

For the next few days Autumn and Bertha were frantically busy, cleaning and polishing and baking.

'Why, Autumn really can cook, Bertha!' Bill exclaimed in mock surprise, as, the day before Thanksgiving, he was allowed to sample an extra pumpkin pie.

'Just for that you don't get it after all!' Autumn told him as she reached for his plate. 'Don't you remember a certain occasion when I cooked the bass for you?'

He gave her a quick look, and just for a moment the atmosphere was electric.

Then the telephone rang. Bill hesitated for an instant before moving towards it.

Autumn didn't see him again until the next afternoon when she was awaiting the arrival of her dinner guests. She had just come out of the kitchen where she had gone to check with Bertha on last-minute preparations, all of which were well in hand, and had come back out into the hall. She paused before the wall mirror to check her hair. Bill suddenly came up behind her, so that his dark face was framed in the mirror above her shining coppery hair, and gazing into the mirror, their glances locked.

'Don't worry,' he said. 'Naquin will find you beautiful, as usual.'

She whirled to face him. 'Will he now?' she asked angrily. 'And what makes you think I care about that?'

'All women want the men in their lives to admire them, don't they?'

'It depends if it's the right man,' she said now, quite seriously.

'Then no problem. Naquin *is* the right man, isn't he?'

Before she could answer or frame a fitting retort, the doorbell rang. Hurt by Bill's attitude, she turned away from him, about to cross the hall and open the door. But he placed a restraining hand on her arm. She paused and turned her head so that she was looking up at him once more. His eyes were dark and serious as he said in a low voice, 'Happy Thanksgiving, Autumn. Your first at Bellefleur. I hope you have many more.'

Now tears stung her eyes at his unexpected words. Her pink lips quivered slightly as she smiled. 'Thank you. Happy Thanksgiving to you, too.'

Together they went to the door to greet their guests.

Everyone gathered in the large, formal parlour that was filled with antiques. Bill had bought some champagne for the occasion, and now, before dinner, they all had a glass as they sat and chatted before the flickering flames in the Italian marble fireplace.

'I do envy you this house, Autumn,' Grace Hebert said. 'I simply adore antiques.'

'So do I,' Marianne Ledet agreed. 'Just imagine living in an old plantation house like this with room after room of beautiful, valuable old things.'

Autumn laughed. 'Actually, sometimes I feel as if I'm living in a museum. Do you know we actually have strangers stop by sometimes and ask to be shown through the house? And say what you will, when you live with furnishings like these'—her hand swept round in an arc, indicating the elegant window hangings, the rosewood piano, the Chippendale tables and crystal chandelier—'you just can't feel quite as at home as you do with modern furnishings. I love it all, but when I want to let my hair down and just be comfortable and inelegant, I head for the library, my bedroom or the kitchen. Bill and I rarely use this room. We usually sit in the library in the evenings if we happen to be at home.'

'I think it's a perfect shame,' Pauline Blanchard said now, 'that Bill's aunt saw fit to leave this place to a stranger. After all,' she added, shrugging delicate shoulders, 'an outsider can scarcely appreciate the historical significance of the house the way a real member of the family can.'

'Yes,' said Marianne Ledet, quickly taking up the conversation in Autumn's defence, 'the same thing happened with your husband's home when he died, didn't it? I understand some of his cousins were quite unhappy about it being willed away from direct descendants, too.'

Pauline's cheeks flushed angrily and Autumn, though she appreciated Marianne's defence, sought frantically in her mind for something soothing to say. Then Bill stepped into the gap. 'Well, naturally Howard left his home to his wife. Any man would. As for Bellefleur, however, I think Aunt Hattie did the wisest possible thing she could when she left it to Autumn. She's really brought this house back to life and the fact is, she's more appreciative of its antiques and its history than I am. And now I think Bertha is ready to serve our dinner,' he ended, and with relief, Autumn looked up to see Bertha signalling from the doorway.

They had scarcely seated their guests and Bill was in the process of carving the turkey when Bertha came into the room and went straight to his side. 'You're wanted on the telephone, Dr Billy,' she said. 'I told him you was about to eat your turkey dinner, but he says it's real important, yes.'

'I'll come,' Bill said at once, standing up and excusing himself before leaving the room. He returned only moments later to say apologetically, 'I'm terribly sorry, but I have to go out on a case. Addie,' he asked, 'would you finish carving the turkey for everyone, please?'

'Oh, Bill!' Pauline wailed. 'How long will you be?' There was a definite droop to her lovely red lips.

He shook his head. 'I'm afraid I can't say. Naturally I'll be back as soon as I can.'

'Can't whoever it is wait until you've at least had your dinner?' she asked impatiently. 'I think it's most inconsiderate, especially since your housekeeper told them you were at the table.'

'I'm terribly sorry,' Bill said again. 'But,' he added more gently, 'they wouldn't have bothered me if it wasn't necessary, you know.'

'I think you allow yourself to be taken advantage of too much,' she complained. 'You need to learn to say no sometimes, Bill, and think of yourself for a change.'

'Please excuse me,' he said formally. He turned to leave and glanced at Autumn with a slight shrug of his shoulders. Then he turned and left the room.

The dinner was a leisurely one. Bertha's rice dressing along with the roasted turkey was a big hit, as were Autumn's pies and home-baked rolls. Everyone seemed to be enjoying themselves except for Pauline, who openly pouted over what she considered Bill's unforgivable lack of good manners.

After dinner, the party returned to the parlour for coffee. 'Dad and your teacher friend seem to have hit it off,' Ellis said with surprise to Autumn as she stood before the fireplace warming her hands. It was the first private words they had had all afternoon.

'I know,' Autumn smiled at him. 'I'm so glad. They're both very nice people.'

'She must be,' Ellis agreed. 'Dad's very particular about whom he likes—especially when it comes to the ladies. I take after him that way. I want only the best.' The tone of his voice altered meaningfully, but Autumn moved away from him to have a word with the mayor's wife. 'Bonnie, would you care for more coffee?' She hoped fervently that Ellis would take the hint that, so far as she was concerned, that subject was as dead as the embers at the bottom of the hearth.

Bill didn't return and, though Autumn was disappointed, she didn't show it. Pauline, however, made it quite clear how she herself felt.

'I just can't understand Bill's attitude,' she complained as she balanced a coffee cup on a saucer in one hand and held a cigarette in the other. 'How he could dare to run away and just desert his guests like this! I'm very, very angry with him!'

'I was under the impression,' Marianne said dryly, 'that we were all Autumn's guests today. She's the one who invited us here.'

'Oh, well, sure,' Pauline acknowledged vaguely. 'But surely she can understand *my* feelings.'

'Of course I do,' Autumn agreed swiftly. 'Bill didn't do this because he's rude,' she said now. 'Someone must really have needed him, otherwise he would have been back by now. I'm sure he'll be home soon.'

But he wasn't back by the time the guests started leaving. Pauline was one of the first to leave. 'Thank heaven,' Marianne sighed before accepting more coffee. 'Talk about a wet blanket!'

But soon even the Ledets were gone, and when Ellis would have stayed on after all the others, Autumn forestalled him. 'I'm rather tired, Ellis,' she told him. 'I think I'll make an early night of it.' And as soon as he was gone, she went upstairs.

It was only about nine and, though she was pleasantly tired, she wasn't sleepy. Bertha's light didn't show beneath her door, so presumably she was asleep. Autumn took pains to move quietly around her own bedroom so as not to wake the housekeeper.

She changed from her dress into a warm, floor-length pale green robe, then she went back downstairs. There she filled in time straightening up the parlour, washing the coffee things and making herself a large cup of hot cocoa.

As soon as she heard the front door she went out into the hall. Bill stood there, shedding his large overcoat. He turned slightly and she saw that he looked absolutely exhausted, worse than he had the night they'd been stranded at the fishing camp. He rubbed a hand wearily across his eyes, then he looked up and saw her standing there.

'I'm sorry,' he apologised, 'about missing your dinner party.'

She shook her head. 'It doesn't matter in the least,' she said quietly. 'But are you all right? You look absolutely worn out.'

'I am,' he admitted. 'It was an Indian woman down the bayou. The only way to reach the place is by boat. They had to come to this side to telephone me and take me to her in a pirogue. She was having a difficult labour.' He paused and wiped his hands over his face again. 'We lost both mother and baby,' he ended hoarsely.

'Oh, Bill!' she cried out. 'I'm so sorry, so dreadfully sorry.'

'So am I,' he said simply. 'Hellishly sorry. The mother was only about sixteen years old, hardly more than a baby herself. And she might not have died if we could have got her to a hospital in time. But by the time I got there she was in too serious a condition to attempt to carry her on foot for about a half a mile and then transfer her into a boat before finally being put into an ambulance. I did everything I knew how for her, but still it wasn't enough.' He bent his head in an agony of distress.

Autumn moved softly across the hall until she was beside him. Gently she touched his arm. 'You did everything you could,' she said quietly. 'You can't reproach yourself, Bill.'

After a moment he lifted his head and nodded. 'I know. But even so, this is something a doctor just never gets used to.'

He fell silent, and Autumn put her hand upon his arm. 'Come out to the kitchen,' she said. 'I've kept your Thanksgiving dinner warm for you.'

CHAPTER TEN

THE month of December simply seemed to fly by, without enough hours to get everything accomplished. In the office, activity picked up as winter 'flu took its toll of the citizens of the community. Outside of office hours, the time was eaten up with Christmas shopping and parties. It seemed to Autumn that everyone in town was throwing a '*petit*' party to celebrate the season and that she was invited to them all. Bill was invited too, of course, but he got out of some of them easily with the excuse of some emergency or other, whether it was real or not. Autumn had no such excuse and she didn't dare risk injuring any feelings by refusing such warm-hearted invitations.

She, Dianne Farland and Bertha worked hard decorating Bellefleur for the season. In the parlour was a gigantic tree which Bill said must be bigger than the one that graced the White House and which took himself and Gary over an hour to wire with lights. Fireplace mantels and stair banisters were festooned with pine boughs and huge red bows. The house took on a scent of fresh pine and enticing things baking in the kitchen.

Two days before Christmas Bill, Autumn, Dianne and Gary all gave a joint party of their own and the old plantation house became bursting with life at this renewed manifestation of gracious hospitality as guest after guest arrived and was served from an abundance of food and drink.

'I'll bet this place was something back in the old days,' Dianne sighed as she paused beside Autumn for a moment in the midst of the throng of guests. 'All the ladies in long, elegant gowns dancing the waltz.'

'I think the ladies look pretty elegant tonight,' Autumn observed. 'We're all wearing long dresses ourselves.' She indicated her own floor-length black velvet gown.

'Yes, but no waltzing,' Dianne pointed out. 'No dancing at all,' she added in disgust. 'Really, Autumn, why didn't we think to hire a combo and move out the furniture and ...'

'Sure,' Autumn laughed. 'And you'd be right out there doing the latest fast steps, huh?' She eyed Dianne's protruding middle beneath a blue, loose-fitting gown.

'Oh, bother!' Dianne exclaimed. 'I feel perfectly fine. Just because I'm pregnant it doesn't mean I can't do things like that.'

'So long as Gary doesn't catch you at it, eh?' Autumn asked.

Dianne grinned. 'Right,' she admitted. Then she sighed. 'I really will be glad when this baby arrives. I'm tired of being treated like spun glass while I look like an elephant.'

'It'll be all over soon,' Autumn comforted her. 'What ... about another four weeks?'

'Yes,' Dianne answered. 'And it can't be too soon for me.' Just then Gary approached her from the other side and, a moment later, Autumn could hear Dianne saying exasperatedly, 'No, I am *not* tired and I don't *feel* like sitting down, Gary.' Autumn grinned to herself and moved away from them in order to mingle with their guests.

Bill was across the room, very good-looking in his dark evening clothes. Autumn's heart tightened at the sight of him. With a sigh, she wondered if she would ever see the day when Bill's presence was met with indifference by herself. As she watched, Pauline, beside him, exquisitely lovely in a soft white dress that emphasised her magnolia complexion, reached up and laid a delicate hand on his arm. Autumn turned quickly, not wanting to be caught watching them, and all but bumped into Ellis, who was close behind her.

'Can I get you a drink?' Ellis offered. 'You look a little tired.'

'Please,' she smiled at him gratefully, 'I'd love it. And I guess I am sort of tired,' she admitted. 'Getting ready for a large party like this is a lot more work than I'd thought it would be, even though I'm enjoying it thoroughly.'

'What time did you get up this morning?' he asked suspiciously.

Autumn laughed. 'Five, and going strong ever since, but please don't tell anybody.'

'No wonder you're dead on your feet,' he said with a frown. 'Go into the library and sit down and prop your feet up. I'll bring your drink to you there.' As she was about to make a protest, he said, 'Only for ten minutes. It'll do you a world of good, Autumn. Robichaux and the Farlands will be in here, they can handle everything for that long. Now, scoot!'

'Well, all right,' she finally agreed reluctantly. She *was* feeling pretty tired, though she hoped nobody would guess how tired. She felt almost as though she could scarcely lift one foot and put it in front of the other. In fact, she couldn't recall ever feeling quite so thoroughly drained before. She would be secretly glad when this evening was over.

She was stretched out on the sofa, eyes closed, and almost asleep, when Ellis came. He was juggling a plate, a glass and the door knob. 'I brought you something to eat as well. I doubt you've had a bite of supper, have you?'

'Well,' she said apologetically as she sat upright and accepted the plate, 'now that you mention it, actually I was too busy. Thanks a million.' She bit into a sausage roll with relish.

'It seems to be a nice party,' Ellis said after a few minutes. 'Everyone appears to be having a good time.'

'I certainly hope so,' she answered. 'I was surprised to see your father come in escorting Grace Hebert. Is there something going on there?'

'I think so,' he said, nodding. 'Dad sees her pretty often. Frankly, I think they want to get married but just haven't quite brought themselves to the point of informing the kid —that's me—just yet. Especially since they haven't known each other very long.'

Autumn laughed. 'And if they do decide to marry, will the kid mind?'

Ellis shook his head. 'Of course not. To tell the truth, I'd be delighted. Dad's a much nicer person having a woman around. He grew kind of hard and cold after my mother died, but lately, he's been different.' He smiled across at her. 'Besides, I'm a grown man,' he told her. 'I have a life of my own to lead, the same as Dad does. All I'm doing is waiting for the go-ahead from a certain girl before I announce to the world that I'm getting married myself.'

'Now, Ellis,' she began protesting. 'You promised me you wouldn't speak of this again and . . .'

'Then I shouldn't have promised,' he said fiercely as he came and sat down beside her. He took the plate from her and placed it on a table, before turning back to her. 'I'm not going to give up until you say you'll marry me, Autumn. I love you too much.'

Before she could possibly move, he had his arms tight around her and his lips were pressed to hers.

The door flew open with a loud crash against the wall without warning and a familiar voice said, 'Please excuse me.'

Autumn wrenched herself from Ellis's embrace. Her face was flaming hot as she looked up reluctantly to meet the coldness on Bill's face.

'You've got a damn nerve!' Ellis blurted out angrily. 'Don't you know how to knock before you enter a room?'

'Sorry,' said Bill, without sounding in the least apologetic, 'but I wasn't expecting to find Autumn in a clinch.' She knotted her hands in her lap as he went on coldly, 'I had thought that as hostess you would be more interested in the welfare of all your guests this evening.'

She stood up on shaky legs. 'I only came in here to rest for a moment,' she said, conscious that her explanation did not sound at all convincing. 'I'll go back to the party now.'

'Don't let him intimidate you, Autumn,' Ellis urged.

'Robichaux's got no right to come in here and start telling you what to do.'

'I agree,' said Bill. His voice was like ice. 'However, I didn't come for that reason.' The expression on his face as he gazed at her arrested Autumn's attention, so that she was suddenly still.

'Why did you come?' she asked tensely.

'There's a new guest,' he told her, looking at her closely. 'A late arrival.'

'Everyone here is as much yours and Dianne's and Gary's guests as mine. Did you really need to seek me out?'

'I think so,' he said implacably. 'This guest claims to be your fiancé.'

'M-my ... my ...' Words failed her as she stared blankly at Bill.

Ellis sounded astounded. 'Autumn's fiancé? What kind of a joke is this?' He turned and glared at Autumn himself.

Bill returned to the hall where he beckoned someone. 'Won't you come in now?'

A moment later he was back in the room, followed by a man Autumn had once known only too well. She looked at him, too stunned even to speak as he came towards her. A moment later Don Prescott, seemingly oblivious of the other two men, swept her limp body into his arms and soundly kissed her on the lips.

'I think'—she heard Bill speak as from a distance, the tone of his voice very dry—'we're in the way, Naquin. Shall we rejoin the party?'

Autumn pulled herself forcibly away from the arms that held her and sucked in a deep, shaky breath. 'What ... what are you doing here, Don?' she asked unsteadily.

He smiled at her warmly. He was as good-looking as ever with his golden blond hair and deep blue eyes. 'What do you think I'm doing here? I've come to be with you for Christmas. I've come to marry you and take you back to New York with me.'

She happened to glance beyond Don's shoulder and met

cold, dark eyes as Bill returned her gaze. Without a word, he turned and strode from the room. Then Ellis's face swam into view and the expression he wore was disbelief and hurt. He, too, turned and left the room.

Only then did Autumn's gaze return to Don. There was a smug, satisfied expression on his face. He opened his arms confidently and held them out, expecting her to step back into them. When she didn't, but instead just stood there silently looking at him, the satisfied look vanished. 'What's the matter?' he asked petulantly. 'Aren't you glad to see me?'

She didn't answer that. Instead she repeated her earlier question. 'Why are you here?'

'I *told* you,' he said, a bit touchily. 'I came to marry you.'

'But I have no intentions of marrying you,' she told him shortly. 'You had no right to tell Bill you were my fiancé!'

'Who, the doc?' Don asked. 'Of course I did. I've got a perfect right to establish my claim—especially to that guy who actually lives here in this house. And I may tell you, Autumn,' he added sourly, 'I don't like that one bit. I know you're doing this just to get back at me, but enough is enough. Now you're going to sell this place and stop acting like a silly ten-year-old and come back home with me where you belong.'

'I'm *not* living with him in the way you mean,' she said stormily. 'We have a housekeeper who lives here, too. So I'm not acting silly *or* like a ten-year-old, and I'm definitely *not* going to marry you. You did me a favour once,' she added tartly, 'when you refused to marry me. Now I'll do us both a favour and do the same.'

'I'm not taking no for an answer, Autumn,' he said obstinately. 'Maybe you've got a right to still be angry with me,' he conceded. 'After all, I realise I was pretty crude. But since you left, I've given it a lot of thought and now I know I'm ready to get married and settle down. With you.'

'How nice!' she snapped. 'But not with me. Now, you're welcome to stay on a few days and spend Christmas with me since you made such a long trip, but only as a friend. My answer is final, Don.'

'I won't believe that,' he told her. 'I'll make you change your mind. You loved me once and I believe you still do, and I don't intend to leave here until you go with me as my wife.'

'I can't discuss this any more tonight,' she said impatiently. 'I've got to return to my guests.' With that, she opened the door and swept out. So far it had been a horrible evening, first with Ellis and then with Don, and with Bill looking on over the whole fiasco. And to top it off, not only was she still tired, she had developed a splitting headache, which was something as a rule she simply never had. She returned to the party and the noisy gaiety with a fixed smile on her face and a prayer that the evening would soon be over so that she could go upstairs and collapse on the bed.

The following morning the headache had dulled, but she still felt listless and achy. She didn't say anything about it, however, when Bill, coming into her bedroom with the usual cup of coffee, looked at her critically and observed, 'You look a bit peaked this morning. You're not getting sick, are you?'

'Of course not,' she assured him quickly. 'I'm just still a bit tired from all the goings on yesterday. Think we'll have many patients this morning?'

Bill shrugged. 'You never can tell on Christmas Eve. Sometimes they come in in droves, getting it over with before I have my holiday, I suppose. Other times, there's only a trickle. Anyhow, you can take this morning off since you have a guest.'

Autumn frowned. She had completely forgotten about Don and his arrival the night before! But she could hardly admit that to Bill, who stood watching her closely. Now she said snappishly, 'I most certainly will not take the morning off. If he can arrive without notice, then he can just entertain himself all morning.'

Bill lifted quizzical dark eyebrows. 'Now that doesn't sound very fiancée-like at all.'

'That's because it isn't,' she said briskly.

'Not?' He looked at her speculatively.

'Not,' she said. She took a sip of the coffee.

'You fell out with him while you were still in New York?'

'I suppose you could say that,' she admitted.

'And now he wants to make it up and marry you.' Are you taking him to the Ledets' party tonight?' he enquired.

Autumn frowned. 'I suppose I'll have to '

'Is Naquin invited as well?'

'Yes.'

He laughed suddenly. 'It ought to be an interesting evening.'

Autumn felt hot tears sting her eyes at his indifferent words. Nothing could have shown her more clearly just how little Bill cared about her than that he could make light of the situation like this.

It was the most horrible Christmas Eve Autumn could recall ever spending. That morning they were inundated with patients at the office. At noon precisely, though, they closed up shop and returned to the main part of the house. Lunch was an awkward affair, shared as it was with the three of them, Don, Bill and herself. Don did not hesitate to show his dislike for Bill, while Bill, for his part, seemed only to be vastly amused. And Autumn felt worse by the minute, and it was a hideous effort to attempt to keep her mind on the conversation at hand. Her headache of the night before had returned full force and she felt more tired than she ever had in her life. All she wanted was the impossible—the opportunity to go to bed and stay there.

The afternoon was even worse. Bill stuck to them like glue, much to Don's glaringly apparent resentment. The three of them walked down to the bayou's edge in the chilling air. Don at last seemed to resign himself to making the best of the situation and asked Bill about local fishing. Bill replied readily and soon was telling the story of the night he and Autumn had spent alone in the fishing cabin. 'It was so cold we really had to do some snuggling to keep warm, didn't we, *chère*?' Autumn gave him a quick look and saw a bland expression on his face.

Don looked livid and Autumn would have been furious, too, if she could only have whipped up the energy. As it was, it really didn't seem to matter that her reputation was taking a beating. At that moment Bill could have shouted from the housetops that they had shared a bed and she wouldn't have raised a finger in protest. She knew he had said what he did simply to anger her and Don.

'Are you all right, *chère*?' he asked easily.

'I'm fine,' she lied. 'Don,' she went on, trying to lighten the atmosphere and take attention away from herself at the same time, 'what do you think of Bertha? Don't you just adore the way she talks? And her cooking? But tomorrow I'll bake the turkey myself. Bertha is going to New Iberia to visit her sister for the day and ... Bill, I thought her sister lived in Lafayette.'

'She's got sisters in both places,' Bill replied, and she was conscious that he was quite aware of how she had tried to change the subject, as they all turned and headed slowly back to the house.

Autumn went through the party that evening at the Ledets on a cloud of pain. There was not a place on her body that didn't seem to ache. Her eyes were dull and weak, her cheeks the unnatural pink that accompanies fever. Several times she caught Bill gazing at her speculatively, but each time she turned away, carefully ignoring him.

Both Don and Ellis vied for her attention throughout the evening, like two bulldogs fighting for a bone. Much of this, however, went right over Autumn's throbbing head. She was too much in a pain-filled world of her own.

She was hardly even aware when Bill finally came over to her and said quietly, 'It's time to go home, Autumn.'

'Maybe she's not ready to go yet,' Ellis said irritably. 'You go ahead. I'll bring Autumn later.'

'Maybe Autumn would prefer to make up her own mind,' Don said with a scowl at Ellis.

'She's dead on her feet and she's going home,' Bill said

firmly. And for once Autumn was thankful for his authoritative, commanding way. She allowed him to take her arm and guide her through the throngs of still celebrating guests to the door and outside into the cold, sharp air.

When the three of them reached the house, Don tried to forestall her from going straight upstairs. 'Let's say goodnight in the library,' he told her. 'I'd like to give you your Christmas present now.'

Bill stood with one foot on the stairs, waiting with a deliberate look of patience.

'Not tonight,' Autumn said agitatedly. 'I really am tired, Don.'

'But, Autumn,' he protested, 'you must . . .'

Then Bill suddenly intervened and took her arm, pulling her towards the stairs. 'Up you go,' he said, and she went gratefully, obedient like a small child.'

The night's sleep didn't bring the hoped-for relief, however. On Christmas morning she awoke feeling worse than ever. Besides the aching body, throbbing head and feverish face she now had a tight, scratchy throat that felt as if it had a rock inside it whenever she tried to swallow. It took an enormous effort to force herself out of bed, but she knew she had to do it. The turkey down in the kitchen was waiting to be baked and breakfast also needed cooking. Bertha would be rushing to try to get away early herself to drive to New Iberia.

She found Bill in the kitchen, as usual looking very much in command of things in his black ribbed sweater and black slacks that hugged his long, lean legs. By contrast, she felt dowdy and plain, wrapped in her long, serviceable but warm green robe, with her over-bright cheeks and watery eyes.

'Morning,' he greeted as she came in. He poured out coffee into two mugs. 'I was just about to come up and bring yours,' he added, indicating one of the mugs. 'Merry Christmas.'

'Merry Christmas,' she greeted back. 'Has Bertha left yet?'

He nodded. 'Half hour ago.'

Autumn headed straight for the refrigerator. 'I've got to get the turkey on to bake,' she said.

'Merry Christmas,' Don spoke from the doorway. Autumn turned towards him, but suddenly he, Bill and the room were fuzzy and unsteady. From a long way off she heard Don say, 'Darling, I want to give you your Christmas present. Can we go somewhere and be alone for a few minutes?' He shot a speaking glance at Bill.

'Not now,' Autumn said, almost sharply. 'I must put the turkey in the oven. And cook breakfast.' Her lip trembled as she thought of all she had to do to prepare their Christmas dinner. It seemed impossibly too much to do.

'Just a few minutes alone,' Don insisted. 'Can't all that wait a few minutes, Autumn? It's important and ...'

At that precise moment things suddenly went black, but not before she was conscious of Bill taking the coffee away from her unresisting fingers.

'B-Bill,' she slurred fuzzily, 'I ... I feel so odd ...' And then the blackness overcame her.

When she came to, she was in her bed and Bill was bending over her. Her eyes were bewildered as she looked up at him. 'What ... what happened?' she asked.

'You fainted,' he said. 'Why didn't you tell me you were ill, Autumn?'

'I ... fainted?' she asked incredulously. 'That's nonsense! I've never fainted before in my life.'

'Well, you just did, and no wonder—all you've been doing while you were sick! How long have you been feeling bad?'

She shrugged slightly. 'Oh, a couple of days, I guess.'

'A couple of ...!' The words sounded like an explosion. 'Why didn't you tell me so I could give you some medication?'

'I don't know,' she said listlessly. 'I suppose I didn't want to make a fuss. There was our party to give, and then Don came and the Christmas dinner to cook and Bertha's trip and ...' Remembrance flooded back. 'I've still got to put the turkey in the oven and start making the dressing.' Agitatedly she made a move to get out of bed. 'I've got so much to do and ...'

His hands pressed her shoulders back down against the white pillows, restraining her. There was a glint of amusement in his eyes. 'You're not going anywhere, *chère*,' he said gently. 'You've got the 'flu and you're going to stay right here in bed until you're over it. I'm going to give you an injection and then you're going to go to sleep and get some rest.'

'But I can't,' she protested half-heartedly, although she knew it was exactly what she wanted to do. 'There's the dinner ... and Don ... and ...'

'Bertha will cook the turkey tomorrow,' Bill assured her, 'so it will only be a day late. As for your boy-friend downstairs, he'll just have to entertain himself, won't he? He can hardly expect you to do so when you're ill. Now go to sleep. I'd better not catch you trying to come downstairs today at all.'

He went out and closed the door quietly but firmly. Autumn stared at the door anxiously. She knew that, despite what Bill said, she ought to make the effort to get up and cook the dinner and see Don, but just now the bed felt so warm and comfortable and her eyelids felt so heavy. She would lie here for ten minutes, she told herself, and rest her eyes. That much time would do wonders, and then she would go downstairs.

She was awakened an hour later by the sound of her door opening. She turned over, opened her eyes and blinked as she tried to orientate herself. Don came into the room and closed the door softly, furtively.

He tiptoed across the floor to the bed and smiled down at her. 'That dragon of a doctor out there seems to regard himself as your keeper and ordered me not to come up here and bother you. But I knew you wouldn't regard *me* as a bother, do you, sweetheart?' He sat down on the edge of the bed and took her hands into his. 'I've been trying to get you alone to myself ever since I arrived. Do you realise this is the first time we've really been alone except for a few minutes that first evening?'

'Don,' she managed now, 'I'm really not feeling at all well. Bill says I've got the 'flu, so maybe you shouldn't be sitting here so close to me.'

'That's just like you, sweetheart,' he said warmly. 'Worrying about me catching your germs. But I'm not concerned. As long as I'm with you, nothing else really matters.' He reached into his jacket pocket and pulled out a small white box. 'I hope you like your Christmas present, sweetheart,' he said as he opened the box to reveal a diamond engagement ring.

'It's beautiful,' she responded automatically but with a noticeable lack of enthusiasm. 'But, Don, I can't . . .' At this point he had the ring out of the box and was attempting to place it on her ring finger on her left hand even as she squeezed the hand into a ball so that he couldn't achieve his objective.

'Don, I . . .' Whatever she had been about to say died as her bedroom door opened once more and Bill stood there, looking darkly at the scene before him. 'I told you,' he said ominously as he advanced into the room, 'not to come up here and bother Autumn.'

Don was clearly disconcerted to be confronted by Bill, but now he blustered, 'I'd hardly call a proposal of marriage "bothering",' as he indicated the ring he held. 'Now if you'll just buzz off, we can get on with this business of getting engaged.'

'I'm afraid it'll have to wait until later,' said Bill in a hard, implacable voice of command. 'Like three or four days. So now, if you don't get out of here, I'm going to put you out myself. Autumn is too ill for a scene of this kind. And if you had an ounce of sense, you'd realise it for yourself.'

Don's face reddened. He turned to Autumn and demanded stiffly, 'What do *you* want, Autumn? Do you want me to go as this . . . this tyrant orders, or do you want me to stay?'

Her head was throbbing so badly through all this that she was practically blind with the pain. It was difficult to speak with her raw, swollen throat. 'Please go, Don,' she pleaded huskily. 'I . . . I really can't seem to think just now. We'll . . . we'll talk later.'

Don stood up abruptly and glared furiously at her. 'Like hell we will!' he spat out viciously. He whirled on his heel and strode hurriedly from the room, slamming the door angrily behind him so that the room vibrated from the blow.

'Oh dear,' Autumn said weakly. Tears pricked her eyes. She felt so helpless and inadequate for straightening anything out or soothing ruffled feelings just now.

Bill seemed quite oblivious of what had happened. 'I'll get some tablets,' he said, and a few minutes later she had swallowed the pills and was back to sleep.

It was only the following morning that she thought to ask about Don, when Bill was cajoling her into drinking an entire glass of orange juice. 'He packed up and left yesterday afternoon,' he said casually, but she was conscious of his eyes upon her as he spoke.

For Autumn, it was a relief.

Bertha was back that day and made some turkey soup which she insisted Autumn drink. 'Dr Billy is a good doctor, *chère*,' she told Autumn, 'and his medicine is good. But this soup is just as good for the 'flu as all those antibiotics, yes. And you have to get some food into you or you'll never get your strength back.' So to please her, Autumn tried.

And whether it was because of Bertha's food, or Bill's antibiotics, or a combination of both, a day came when Bill allowed her out of bed and permitted her to go downstairs for dinner. She dressed in a softly flowing long hostess gown in a rust colour that blended with her hair. She still felt a little shaky and her face was pale enough that it needed a little help from cosmetics, but even so, the sparkle of life was once more back in her eyes.

She saw Bill smile welcomingly when she descended the stairs and reached the hall. Together they went into the dining room where the table was laid for two. White candles flickered on the table on each side of a centrepiece of golden chrysanthemums and vivid red poinsettias. Bill pulled Autumn's chair out and she was seated.

Then she noticed a gaily-wrapped package on her plate, and looked across at him questioningly. 'Your belated Christmas present,' he said. 'Others are still under the tree, but I wanted to give you mine now.'

She opened it and discovered a beautiful glowing diamond pendant on the daintest gold serpentine chain she had ever seen. She lifted her dark lashes and her eyes met his, troubled. 'It's beautiful,' she said softly. 'But, Bill, I can't take anything as valuable as this.'

He smiled and reached over and covered her trembling hand with his. 'Certainly you'll take it,' he said firmly. 'Call it a friendship gift. And we are friends, aren't we?' She felt his eyes upon her.

'Well, yes, of course, but . . .'

'No buts,' he commanded. 'Here, let me put it on for you.' But when she continued to look thoughtful and worried, he frowned slightly. 'Just look upon it as my way of saying that I no longer resent your coming here and inheriting Bellefleur. That, in fact, I'm glad you're here. Okay?'

She nodded at last, but her heart was heavy as she forced a smile to her lips. Bill's words could mean so much if he only returned her love. But a man didn't give a 'friendship gift' to a girl he loved.

Even so, as her fingers traced the delicate design of the necklace that now hung between her breasts, she knew it was a gift she would cherish for the rest of her life.

CHAPTER ELEVEN

THE following morning Autumn gazed at her reflection in the bedroom mirror with unhappy eyes. The necklace Bill had given her winked and flickered against her skin as it caught the light. It was a beautiful piece of jewellery and she ought to be grateful that he had thought enough of her to give it to her. But, in truth, the sight of it ony served to make her more miserable than ever, even though, perversely, she treasured it. Last night he had emphasised that it was friendship that had prompted him to give it to her. Generous friendship, true, but friendship all the same.

She wondered if he had given Pauline an engagement ring for Christmas and if they would announce a wedding date soon. It was a possibility that hurt deeply even to contemplate, but she knew she must steel herself against such an eventuality.

Ellis telephoned a number of times during her recuperation, but Don was silent. Now that she was recovered and on her feet again, she felt rather badly about him. True, she was finished with him for good—had been even before he came, but still, a man who travelled a thousand miles to propose deserved better than being banished from the object of that proposal without any consideration. So she sat down and wrote him a letter of apology, at the same time making it plain that there was no possibility now or in the future of her ever accepting his proposal.

During the week after New Year, she returned to work in the office, and she felt that Bill was glad to have her back. 'It's been a nightmare around here,' he told her. 'I've had appointments mixed up and somehow the filing system has gone to pot.' Autumn supposed wryly that at least she was valuable to Bill in some capacity, even if not quite the way she wanted.

A few afternoons later Marianne called in just at closing time and together they went into the house. Bertha obligingly served them coffee and cake even as she scolded, 'Don't eat too much of that cake, no, Automne, or you'll spoil your appetite for your supper.'

Marianne laughed as Bertha retreated from the parlour, where they were seated. 'She acts as though she were your mother instead of your housekeeper!'

Autumn laughed, too. 'I know. It's kind of a nice feeling, actually, especially since I was ill. I guess I'm still weak enough to enjoy a bit of mothering.'

Marianne eyed her keenly. 'You look as though you've been through the washer. There are still some blue smudges beneath your eyes that weren't there before. I hear from the grapevine that your fiancé went off in a huff on Christmas Day just because you came down sick. Any truth in it? Addie got the story at a café in town where Don stopped for a meal on his way out of town.'

Autumn was relieved to know that Bill hadn't been gossiping and that no one apparently knew the real story. Now she shook her head. 'It wasn't quite like that,' she said. 'And it's just as well he left—I was too sick to be any company to him. And he's not my fiancé.'

'Well, I'm glad to hear that,' said Marianne. 'I'd rather hate to lose you back to New York since we've got to be friends.' The subject was dropped then and Marianne went on to talk about Mardi Gras which would be coming up next month. 'I've got to drive to New Orleans next week,' she said, 'to check on how the costumes are coming along for the Royal Court.'

'Are you the Queen?' Autumn asked. She had only a hazy idea of what Mardi Gras was all about.

Marianne laughed. 'Oh, no indeed! The Krewe here in St Pierre always has a young unmarried girl who's a daughter of a member. But this year Addie is the King, so naturally I'm involved up to my ears. I was Queen the year after I graduated from high school.'

'Is Bill going to be on the Court, too?' Autumn found herself asking.

'Oh, no. He's not even a member of the club. He says he's too busy to have the time to get involved with Carnival, but he usually manages to attend our ball. You will too, this year, of course. I'll see that you have a ticket for a seat in the reviewing stand for the parade and a ticket for the ball as well.'

'Thanks,' said Autumn. 'It does sound like fun.'

The weather stayed cold—and to Autumn it seemed as though it were always raining. In its own way, it was as bad as the snow one had to contend with back East. And this damp, penetrating cold was different, too; it seemed to work right through one's skin straight to the bones.

Now that she was well again she was back full swing in her busy life. Besides her work in the office she helped Marianne with church work, Grace with her home economics girls and Dianne with the finishing touches to the nursery. Over the holidays while school was closed, Gary had painted the spare bedroom in their apartment a pale sunshine yellow and Dianne had sewed gaily-printed curtains that boasted green giraffes and yellow elephants and a multitude of equally improbable flowers and birds. Autumn secretly purchased and painted white a wicker rocking-chair, and Dianne was so delighted she immediately sewed a cushion for it that matched the nursery curtains.

Autumn did all Dianne's shopping now, too, whenever Gary was unavailable for the task. The weather was so consistently bad that both of them had begged Dianne not to go out and take any chances. The baby wasn't due for another two or three weeks and she was in excellent health, but she was large and heavy and it would be just too easy for her to slip and fall on a slippery concrete sidewalk, so they convinced her that they weren't being overly protective.

Dianne was also not allowed to attend any ball games. While Gary had been assistant football coach in the fall, he was now head basketball coach, so this kept him busily occupied. Dianne chaffed at the bit to be allowed to go to the games, but Gary put his foot down. 'I need to have all my concentration on the game, honey,' he told her. 'And if you were there, I'd be worried about how you were feeling. It's just getting too close to countdown.' So at last she had to give in, although with less grace than she had over the shopping subject, and agreed to spend basketball evenings in Autumn's company.

One rainy morning Bertha came through the connecting door from the house into the office. Autumn knew at once that something was wrong because this was a thing Bertha simply never did. She stood up at once and went towards the other woman, who had stopped at the door. 'What is it, Bertha?' she asked in a hushed voice that couldn't carry to waiting patients.

'It's my sister in Lafayette,' Bertha said in great agitation, as she twisted her apron in her hands. 'The one that had the operation a few months ago. She just called on the telephone. Her husband had a heart attack this morning, and he's in bad shape. And my sister, she wants me to come at once to be with her.'

'Well, of course she does,' Autumn agreed at once. 'Let's tell Bill and he'll just have to cover the office himself while I help you pack. Are you taking the bus?'

Bertha nodded. 'I'll need to call for a schedule, yes.'

'I'll do that for you,' Autumn said soothingly, 'and drive you to the bus station when it's time.'

An hour later she stood in the pouring rain and waved to Bertha, who peered out and waved back from behind a window inside the bus. Then she flipped up the collar of her raincoat and turned with a sigh and sloshed through the water back to where the car was parked.

By late afternoon the rain had slackened off and the radio announcer promised that the weather bureau had assured

them that the outlook was set fair. 'Still,' Dianne pointed
out as she sat in the kitchen watching Autumn prepare
dinner, 'the roads are wet and slippery. I wish Gary didn't
have this out-of-town game. I was hoping they'd call it off
because of the weather.'

'I suppose they would have if the rain hadn't stopped,'
Autumn said. Since Gary was to be gone for the evening
she had invited Dianne to have supper with her and Bill as
well as to spend the remainder of the evening with them
until Gary returned. She dropped a dollop of butter on to
the potatoes and began vigorously mashing them. 'Check the
biscuits in the oven, will you, Dianne? They should be just
about done.'

Bill came in a minute or so later and Autumn set the
kitchen table for the three of them after a unanimous vote
that they preferred the cosy warmth of the kitchen to the
formal chilliness of the dining room. 'But don't tell Bertha
I served a guest in the kitchen,' Autumn laughed as they sat
down. 'She'd be horrified at my lack of manners!'

The three of them chatted easily during the meal, and
afterwards Bill helped Autumn do the washing up, both of
them refusing to allow Dianne to help.

They had just finished with the kitchen when the rain
started again. 'Well, would you just look at that!' Dianne
exclaimed in disgust. 'We're all going to have to grow
webbed feet if this keeps up!'

'That's the truth,' Bill agreed. The telephone rang and,
with a groan, he went out of the room, saying, 'Wouldn't
you know ... somebody needs me to come out on a night
like this. I sure was looking forward to propping my feet
up in the library and taking it easy.'

Autumn looked after him with sympathetic eyes, but
there was nothing she could do to help him. She turned
back to Dianne and asked, 'Well, what shall we do with ourselves tonight? Television? A card game?'

'To be honest,' said Dianne, 'my back is aching a little.
Would you mind if we went back to my apartment and I got

into bed? I mean, we could just visit and talk in there, couldn't we?'

'Of course,' Autumn agreed at once. 'I'll just tell Bill.'

She caught him just as he was about to go out of the door, carying his black medical bag. 'Think you'll be late getting back?' she asked.

He shrugged. 'I hope not. I'm dog-tired today.'

She looked at him anxiously and then out of the door at the driving rain. 'Be careful,' she told him quietly. 'If you're going to be late after all, call me so I won't worry, will you?'

He gazed at her intently. 'You'd worry?'

'Of course I'd worry,' she exclaimed. 'This weather isn't fit for ducks, much less humans!'

'Autumn——?' His eyes, despite his tiredness, had a curious light in them, but before he could add whatever he had been about to say, Dianne walked into the hall and joined them. Then Bill was gone, leaving Autumn wondering what he had been going to say.

She and Dianne spent a quiet evening talking about the coming baby and discussing possible names for it. Bill returned around nine and came to the bedroom door to announce his presence, then went back to the main part of the house with the intention of watching television for a while.

It was around eleven when Dianne asked, 'What time do you think the bus will return? The game must have been over a good long time by now.'

'It's also raining cats and dogs,' Autumn reminded her. 'If the bus is able to make it through at all, I imagine it's creeping along about two miles an hour.'

There came a tapping at the bedroom door and Autumn rose and went quickly to it. It was Bill and he beckoned Autumn out, so she smiled at Dianne and said, 'Be right back. Bill wants to speak to me.'

When her gaze returned to Bill, a strange apprehension filled her. His face was drained of all colour, his eyes dark, muddy pools. He was wearing a bright yellow rain slicker and for the second time that evening he was carrying his medical bag. 'What is it?' she whispered apprehensively as they stepped into the Farlands' living room, a safe distance from being overheard from the bedroom.

'The bus carrying the basketball team had an accident,' he said grimly. 'I just got the call.'

'Oh, my God!' she exclaimed in a low voice. 'How bad?'

He shook his head. 'From the sound of it, pretty bad,' he told her frankly. 'I'm leaving now to go out there. The sheriff has alerted the hospitals in Houma and New Orleans and they're sending ambulances.'

'Where did it happen?' she asked, following him down the hallway as he headed for the door.

'About ten miles west of town.' He paused and looked at her soberly. 'I'll call and let you know about Gary the instant I possibly can. What are you going to tell her?' he asked, nodding back in the direction of the apartment they had just left.

'Nothing if I can help it,' she decided. 'But she's already worrying about the bus being late.'

He nodded again. 'Stall her as much as possible ... at least until you know something definite. Well ...' He broke off as he opened the door. They could clearly hear the flood outside as it assaulted the porch roof and ground. 'Take care,' Autumn called after him as he ran out into the hammering rain.

Her heart felt as though it was in the pit of her stomach as she went slowly back down the hallway and into the Farlands' apartment. How on earth was she ever going to get through the night, keeping Dianne calm and free from worry, knowing what she did? It was an impossible task and she felt far too inadequate to cope.

'What did Bill want?' Dianne asked curiously as Autumn entered the bedroom.

Autumn shrugged, trying to appear casual and unconcerned. 'He just wanted to tell me he has to go out again.'

'Poor Bill,' Dianne sympathised. 'Tonight of all nights, in weather like this, he keeps getting called out. And he was so tired already at supper that ... listen,' she cut off sharply as she pointed to the television set. The newscaster was giving a late bulletin on the storm. They listened in silence until it was over and Dianne exclaimed, 'One bridge out and another flooded, both leading out of St Pierre! Oh, I hope Gary is safe. Surely the bus has stopped somewhere for the night, don't you think, Autumn?' she appealed. 'They wouldn't try to drive all the way home through this, would they? But in that case, why hasn't he telephoned me?'

'Maybe there are some telephone wires down, too,' Autumn suggested, feeling a deep gratitude that so far news of the accident had not yet reached the TV stations for broadcast. 'There are some pretty strong winds with this storm.' As if to emphasise her words, they heard a crack and a thud not far from the house. They looked at one another in fear, but Autumn quickly resumed her outwardly calm demeanour for Dianne's sake. 'Must have been a tree branch falling.'

'I guess so,' Dianne agreed. 'I hope you're right about why Gary hasn't called or come. I am *trying* not to worry,' she added with a brave smile on her face.

'Good girl,' Autumn smiled back. 'Now, do you want to watch the late show ... my, the TV interference is awful,' she observed as she looked at the snowy, flickering picture. 'I'll switch the channel and see if ...' A sudden groan jerked her head around. 'Dianne!'

Dianne's hands were spread over her protruding mid-section and there were beads of perspiration on her forehead that hadn't been there a moment ago. 'Sorry,' she said now, a little breathlessly. 'Another of those false labour contractions, I guess. For the past month I've been having them off and on—although I must say never quite that strong.'

'Now look, Dianne,' Autumn said severely, 'you simply *cannot* have that baby tonight, what with Bill and Gary both away and bridges washed out so that there's no way to reach a hospital! I don't know the *first* thing about childbirth, so keep that in mind, will you?'

Dianne grinned and brushed a strand of long, silky hair

away from her face. 'Don't worry,' she said reassuringly. 'The baby isn't due for another two weeks.'

'Have you told that to him?' Autumn asked as she pointed a finger at Dianne's middle. Dianne giggled and Autumn turned again to the television set, trying to bring in more clearly a hopelessly jumpy picture.

Forty-five minutes later Autumn conceded to herself that the baby was in earnest. She rushed to the telephone, knowing she couldn't reach Bill but hoping at least to reach Marianne or someone else who could help. To her utter dismay, she discovered the telephone line was dead.

She sucked in a ragged breath and wasted an entire two minutes in pure unadulterated panic before she returned to the bedroom once again.

And Dianne didn't help matters. She kept crying, 'I want Gary here!' And Autumn had her hands full trying to keep her calm.

There was no telling at all when Bill would be able to return. Promising Dianne that she would return shortly, she shrugged into a raincoat and galoshes and, picking up a flashlight, went outside into the storm and down the drive to check the bayou. The driving rain and wind almost bent her double as she pushed against it.

When she reached the bayou, what she saw made her heart sink, although rationally it was only what she had by now expected. The bayou had swollen until the water level had risen to swish over the edges of the bridge. It would be dangerous in the extreme to attempt to drive across it now. Which meant that she and Dianne could not get out and no one else could get in. For the remainder of this night, at least, and maybe even tomorrow, they were on their own, effectively cut off from the rest of the world.

She bit her bottom lip nervously and then turned and ran, stumbling and sliding, back to the house. She shed her rain gear and hurried again to Dianne's bedroom, knowing the other girl must be frightened at being left totally alone, even for only these few minutes.

'What's it like?' Dianne asked anxiously, lifting her heavy

body slightly up from the bed so that she could watch Autumn as she towelled her hair dry.

'We're marooned,' Autumn told her bluntly. 'The bridge is already impassable. That means that neither Gary nor Bill can get in here tonight and we can't get you out to a hospital. We've got to do this thing alone, honey,' she added, trying to sound brave and self-confident, while inside she was quaking with dread and fear.

Dianne's lips trembled slightly. 'I can't believe,' she said shakily, 'that we moved into a house with a doctor living in it and now when I need him the doctor is gone, Gary is gone——' her voice quivered dangerously, 'the phone is out, the bridge is flooded and even Bertha is away. It sounds like a bad play, Autumn!' she ended with a little laugh.

Autumn smiled tremulously. 'I know it does,' she agreed. 'I'll be glad when it's all over, won't you? Now,' briskly, 'do you think I ought to go and boil some water?'

Dianne giggled, showing a little of her former cheerfulness. 'What on earth *do* they do with all that boiled water?' she asked now.

'Keep the husband busy,' Autumn laughed. The laugh was cut off by another groan from Dianne. She rushed to the girl's side and gripped her hands tightly in her own. She frantically searched her memory for all the information she had ever heard and perhaps tucked away concerning delivering babies. She knew there was the umbilical cord to tie, the afterbirth to be dealt with, but what else? What else? She felt so ignorant, so inadequate.

'I think it's getting ready to come!' Dianne gasped breathlessly.

Autumn threw back the bedcovers, checked and said, 'I think you're right. Now, next contraction, bear down hard, okay?'

From then on she didn't have time to give a spare thought to her fears, the storm that was still raging or to Bill and the accident victims. She was far too busy dealing with the demanding reality of here and now. She was only aware of the young girl lying on the bed who needed her and completely depended on her.

Towards dawn, with the storm abating its relentless fury at last, Diane's infant son took his first gasping breath as Autumn held the tiny body in her two hands.

'We did it!' she exultantly told an exhausted Dianne. 'You have a wonderful little boy.' She took a clean baby blanket and wrapped it round the small form and laid him gently in the crook of his mother's arms. 'I'll give him a bath in a little while,' she said. 'But you and I have a tiny bit of work left to do.'

Around ten that morning, while mother and child both slept, an exhausted Autumn went outside on to the now sunwashed veranda and surveyed the sodden grounds, the broken tree limbs that cluttered the lawn. She wondered about the bayou and whether its waters were still up over the bridge, but she didn't walk down to check—it was just more effort than she could summons at the moment. Instead she dropped into a porch chair and stared unseeingly at the lawn and trees, her thoughts worried and sober. She now had time to wonder how many injured there had been in that bus accident—and whether Gary was one of the victims.

Dianne had been too worn out herself to mention Gary again after the baby had been born, but when she awakened later, she would most certainly be demanding her young husband's presence again. *And what*, Autumn wondered dismally, *can I tell her*? I can't put her off indefinitely.

She closed her eyes wearily and had almost dozed off to sleep on the veranda when the sound of an automobile suddenly jerked her awake. She leaned forward in her chair, alert, tensed, and a moment later Bill's L.T.D. swept into view and the tires came swishing to a stop on the wet drive.

Autumn rose and ran down the steps as Bill and Gary Farland both got out of the car and came towards her.

'Thank God!' she said fervently. The two men looked dirty and wet and even more exhausted than she. There were dark smudges beneath Bill's eyes and somehow, in the past long night, Gary had lost his youth and gaiety and become a grim, unsmiling man. 'It was ... that bad?' she asked jerkily.

Bill nodded tiredly. 'That bad. Three of the boys on the team died and five more are in a critical condition. Seven others are in hospital with broken limbs or ribs. It's only a miracle Gary here is even alive, much less not even hurt. The bus driver is in bad shape himself.'

'I was thrown from the bus,' Gary told her, 'on to a soft shoulder of the road. 'I was barely scratched.' He rubbed a hand across the nightmare vision his eyes still held. Then he looked at Autumn again. 'I suppose Dianne is hysterical?'

Autumn shook her head and despite the grim news the men brought, despite everyone's total exhaustion, a twinkle of joy stole back into her eyes, but she kept her lips straight. 'She doesn't know about the acident,' she acknowledged. 'I told her the bus had probably stopped somewhere for the night to wait out the storm. But come with me. I want you to see what she's been doing while you've been gone.'

She led the two men quickly into the house and down the hall and into Dianne's bedroom. Then she glanced up at Gary as he came to a stop at the foot of the bed. His eyes rested with sudden and unexpecteded tenderness on the picture of his wife and child sleeping peacefully. Autumn saw his Adam's apple bobbing in his throat as he sought to get a grip on his emotions.

Just at that moment Dianne opened her eyes and cried out joyfully, 'Gary!'

'Darling!' Gary moved round the bed to his wife's side and, as he bent towards her, Bill touched Autumn's arm and led her away, softly closing the bedroom door behind them.

In the large hall back in their own part of the house, Bill stopped her and put both his hands on Autumn's shoulders. 'So you did all that by yourself?' he asked.

A smile of her own peeped out. 'Well,' she allowed, 'I suppose you *could* say I had a little help from Dianne, too.'

He shook his head wonderingly. 'And I once thought you were too beautiful to be useful!'

For the next week life was so hectic, Autumn rarely saw Bill at all. Each day he visited hospitals in both Houma and New Orleans, checking on all the local boys who had been injured. He left very early in the morning for one visit and would take the other trip late in the afternoons. In between, the office was packed with patients as usual and also simply folks who wanted the latest news on the boys' conditions. Bill was very patient in his dealings with each and every one of them.

But finally life showed signs of settling down again. Bill announced to Autumn one morning that he wouldn't be making his daily trips to New Orleans and Houma any longer. Some of the boys had been released from the hospitals, some were there for a long stay, but were now out of the wood as far as life or death was concerned, so Bill was now leaving them in the care of their various specialists and felt they no longer needed the reassurance of their local family physician's presence each day. Autumn was glad. Bill looked so dreadfully tired all the time these days and there was a pinched, set look around his mouth. He needed rest badly.

Pauline reached the same conclusion when she arrived for an unexpected visit one afternoon just at closing time. 'You've been working yourself to the point of exhaustion,' she scolded him when he joined her in the waiting room. She linked her arms around his and smiled up at him. 'Now I absolutely insist that you come out to my place tonight for dinner. It'll do you good. You need a rest and a change of scenery and . . .'

Autumn heard no more because she had quietly got up and headed for the door that led into the house. She was giving Bill no opportunity whatsoever of accusing her of eavesdropping, even if they *had* been talking openly standing right in front of her desk.

Fifteen minutes later Bill poked his head into the kitchen where Autumn was sitting at the table, resting with a cup of coffee and trying to decide whether she should cook for one or for two. The question was soon answered when Bill said, 'I won't be in for dinner tonight, so you don't have to bother about me.'

She nodded automatically, and it was only after he left that the tears spilled over.

The next day was Saturday and when she and Bill closed up the office at noon she could only think, as she watched him, that he didn't look any more rested from his evening at Pauline's than he had before.

He followed her back into the house and seemed to echo her thoughts. 'I really need a break,' he said now. 'A complete change. Why don't we run over to New Orleans this afternoon? We'll visit the French Market and the St Louis Cathedral and ride the trolley, and tonight we'll go somewhere for dinner and dancing.' His glance held hers. 'Well, what do you say?'

She ached to be able to accept. When he was like this it was so very hard to keep a distance, to keep up a veneer of indifference. But to spend a day and an evening with him, just the two of them alone, was more than she could stand. She had discovered how difficult that was when they had been stranded together in the fishing cabin. To be alone like that with him for hours would mean she would have to guard every glance, be careful of every word, and somehow she felt more vulnerable these days than she had in the past. What if she wasn't able to keep her emotions under tight control? If Bill ever found out the truth about how she felt, they would not be able to go on sharing the same roof. So she shook her head and said, 'Thank you for the offer, but I think I'll pass.'

His eyes narrowed as he gazed at her with a blunt directness. 'You don't want to go?'

Thinking of Pauline, of the two of them together last night, made it easier to shake her head again. 'No,' she lied now, with her fingers superstitiously crossed behind her so that he couldn't see, 'I don't think so today.'

'Do you have any other plans?' he demanded.

'Not really,' she answered in desperation. 'But I just really don't feel like making the effort that such a big day out would require.'

'In other words, you just don't want to go out with me,' he said in a hard, cold voice. 'That's the real truth, isn't it? Isn't it?' he demanded insistently.

'Yes.' The word came out in a ragged whisper.

'You don't need to tell me twice,' he said harshly. Then he wheeled round and strode purposefully out of the door while Autumn pressed her doubled fist against her lips to stifle a cry. She wanted to run after him, to erase that hard, angry look from his face. She longed to tell him the truth .. that she loved him and wanted to spend all her days with him, but she stayed still. It was better to let him go. Because so long as he was angry with her and stayed away from her, he wouldn't be as likely to discover her secret.

CHAPTER TWELVE

'THERE is a Mr Chaisson waiting to see you, Doctor.'

'Thank you, Miss McBride,' Bill said to her in a cold, formal voice. 'I'll be there in just a moment.' He removed his hand from the telephone receiver which he had covered when she entered the office. 'What did you say, Pauline? Oh, that was only the office girl bringing me a message. I'm afraid I'll have to go now. I . . .'

Autumn gently pulled the door shut behind her and went back to her own desk. Hot tears burned her eyes and she blinked rapidly to keep them from falling. *That does it*, she told herself, suddenly making up her mind. She would leave Bellefleur, leave St Pierre, leave Louisiana and go back where she belonged. It was something she should have done long ago, but she had been too stubborn to admit it. *The office girl*, indeed! As though she had no name, no identity at all as far as he was concerned. That, more than anything, proved to her finally and irrevocably that by staying she was merely postponing the inevitable.

Ever since that day, almost two weeks ago, when he had invited her to New Orleans and she had refused, things had been cold and strained between them. No longer did Bill arrive at her bedroom door each morning with a mug of strong coffee. No longer did they share their meals in the large, formal dining room. Now he took his meals in the kitchen or not at all, vanishing often at mealtimes, so that Autumn suspected he spent those times at Pauline's. In the office they were as they had been a few moments ago, chillingly polite and formal. Bertha, who had returned a week ago from her sister's, once her brother-in-law was on the mend at last, was openly baffled at their behaviour. 'You

172

have a lovers' quarrel, you two?' she demanded bluntly of Autumn.

Autumn's face had heated beneath the older woman's piercing eyes. 'We're not lovers, so how would we have a lovers' quarrel?'

'Hmmmph,' Bertha grunted, making no comment to that. 'The air in this ole houe is definitely cold, cold, and I'm not talking 'bout the weather, no.'

Autumn sighed wearily. 'Let's just say we're not friends any more and leave it at that, shall we?'

But now as she sat at her desk in the waiting room, she faced the fact that not only were they no longer friends, they were the next thing to enemies, and before the situation could deteriorate to that point, she would leave here.

Miraculously, it was a slow afternoon as far as patients were concerned, and step by step, she planned things out. There were only two more weeks until Mardi Gras and she considered that it would be a real shame to come and live in south Louisiana this many months and then leave without attending their crowning celebration of the year, Carnival. It would disappoint Marianne, too. Besides which, she herself really wanted to be here for it. So she decided that she would stay two more weeks and then head back east the day following Mardi Gras.

She would have to make arrangements about Bellefleur. But that, surely, was easily accomplished. She picked up the telephone and called Mr Naquin, Ellis's father, and made an appointment with him for late that same afternoon, as soon as she could get there after they had closed up the medical office.

That left only one thing more to do, so she did it. She rolled a piece of paper into the typewriter. Ten minutes later she pulled it out and took it in to Bill's private office and placed it on his desk. She was careful to wait until he was in the lab, so that he wouldn't see her. Then, as it was now five o'clock, she grabbed her handbag and went outside to her car.

'What can I do for you?' Mr Naquin enquired a few minutes later, as he stood up and shook hands with her across the desk. 'Not in any legal trouble, I hope?'

'No. Mr Naquin, when I first inherited Bellefleur, you explained that I couldn't sell the house for five years. But tell me this—is there any restrictions against my giving it away?'

Mr Naquin blinked. 'Give?'

She nodded.

He coughed and took his eyeglasses off in order to polish them with his handkerchief. 'Well,' he said slowly, after some deliberation, 'I suppose there isn't. I guess Miss Hattie never gave any thought to the possibility that you might want to do that. And to whom,' he added now, 'do you plan to give it?'

'Bill Robichaux,' she said promptly. 'By rights Bellefleur as well as its lands should be completely his. And now, as I've decided to return to New York, I felt it was best to get this matter settled before I go.'

'You're returning to New York for good?'

'Yes. In two weeks' time, just after Mardi Gras. So could you possibly tie up all the legal ends of this for me before then, sir? So that there can be no question about its being his?'

'Yes, of course, my dear. But have you considered this matter thoroughly? After all, in five years' time you could sell it and make a little nest egg from it.'

She shook her head. 'No. I want to do it this way.'

'Then, if you're quite definite, I'll have the papers drawn up tomorrow.'

'Thank you.' Autumn smiled now, though there was a big knot in her throat at the thought of giving up Bellefleur for good, and the fact that it meant she would never see her beloved house or its new and rightful owner again in only a few short weeks. She wasn't sure how she was actually going to face up to that fact when the time came, but at least she felt assured that she was doing the right, the only honourable thing to do, about Bellefleur.

She left the office and went outside in the nearly dark evening. Just as she was about to get into her car, she saw Ellis getting out of his and striding purposefully towards her. 'Hello,' he said with a pleased smile. 'I thought it was you.' He glanced at the brick building behind her. 'Were you looking for me?' he asked hopefully.

She smiled and shook her head. 'Actually, it was your father I came to see. I've just left him. I had a little ... business to attend to.'

'Well,' said Ellis, entirely uncurious as to her business, 'if it's taken care of, how about having dinner with me to-night?'

Her first instinct was to say no, but then she thought it would be a good time to tell him that she was moving back East. She'd rather tell him herself than have him find out from someone else, so now she suddenly nodded. 'Fine. But I need to go home and take a shower and change first.'

'Pick you up at seven-thirty,' he told her.

When, ten minutes later, she entered the front hall at Bellefleur, Bill came out from the open library. His face was sober, even a bit grim, as he stood gazing at her. 'Would you come into the library, please?' he asked in an impersonally polite voice. 'I'd like a word with you.'

So, after all, he had discovered her letter of resignation on his desk. She had hoped he wouldn't find it until morning so that she would have a night in which to think up answers to the questions he was bound to ask. But now there was no time for that. She nodded as she unbuttoned her grey wool coat and draped it across the banister. Wordlessly she entered the library before him.

Bill closed the door, shutting out the cold draught of the hall so that the room would retain the warmth of the fire that glowed in the hearth. Autumn went to stand before the flames and held out her hands to its warmth, more as an excuse not to have to face Bill than from any real need of the heat.

Obviously this incited him, because now he came forward and shook her letter in her face. 'Just what is the meaning of this?' he asked in a cold voice in which violent anger was just barely suppressed.

'It ... it means just what it says,' she answered a little nervously. 'I'm resigning my job.'

'For what reason?' he demanded now. Sarcastically, he added, 'You neglected to clarify that.'

Now, uneasily, she moved away from him and the fire and around a large, overstuffed chair. 'Is it necessary that you have a reason?' she asked. 'Isn't it enough that you've got my resignation?'

'No, damn it, it is not!' he exploded. He threw her letter deliberately into the annihilating flames and strode rapidly round the chair that separated them until he was standing only inches away from her. 'That,' he waved an angry hand in the direction of the fireplace, 'is where a piece of nonsense like that belongs.'

Now she was angry at him for not taking her seriously. 'Then I'll just write another! And another!' She stopped and for a long moment they stood glaring at one another without speaking.

Then Bill ran long, sensitive fingers through his rich dark hair. 'Then you really mean it,' he said at last.

'Yes, of course.'

'Why?'

'Because I'm going back to New York as soon as Mardi Gras is over. I'll continue working for you until then.'

His eyes were dark storms again. 'So you're going back to marry that guy after all?' he all but sneered.

'Yes,' she agreed at once. It was the perfect answer— for him to think she was going to marry Don. Why hadn't she thought of that herself? It gave Bill a believable answer and somehow it salvaged a bit of her bruised pride, too, having him think that. This way, he wouldn't be so likely ever to guess the real truth. 'Yes,' she said again, 'I'm going back to marry Don.'

'And you think you'll be happy with him?' he demanded.

'You didn't think so at one time or else you wouldn't have run away from him and come to Louisiana.'

She shrugged, feigning indifference. 'People change. And yes, I think I'll be content.'

'I said happy, not content,' he pointed out obstinately.

She gazed at him helplessly. Now she was feeling the tears clogging her throat again. 'Is anyone ever really happy these days?' she countered. 'I don't ask for happiness. I only ask for contentment.'

'How dull!' he snapped harshly. 'And what a hell of a thing to warm you on a cold winter's night.'

Autumn's face burned at that and she turned away from him. 'I don't need to stand here and have you hurl insults at me.' She only took a couple of steps towards the door, however, before he gripped her arm roughly and stopped her.

'What about Bellefleur?' he asked now. 'Will you sell it to me after the five-year restriction is lifted?' His voice was cold, chipped, precise. And absolutely demanding.

'No,' she said, equally coldly. 'I will never sell Bellefleur to you! Never!'

His piercing eyes were almost like poison daggers as his anger darted at her. 'Well, thank you,' he said with heavy sarcasm, 'for your kind consideration.' Then he brushed past her and went out the door, leaving her to stare after him, hurt and miserable and utterly bewildered.

Three hours later she was unhappily having another trying scene with Ellis in his car in the Country Club parking lot. 'But, Autumn, you can't go back to New York,' he was saying. 'There's nothing there for you. Unless . . . but you're not going back to marry that guy who was here, are you?'

She shook her head. This was Ellis, not Bill, and there was no need for pride to lie here. 'No,' she told him truthfully, 'I'm not going to marry him.'

'Then why go?' he asked. 'You know I love you—that I'd do anything to make you happy if only you'd marry me. Autumn, please . . .'

She lifted a hand and touched his lips gently to silence

him. 'I'm sorry, Ellis,' she told him quietly. 'But it would never work. I just don't love you.'

He eyed her glumly. 'You told me once that you were in love with someone who didn't love you. When that guy came down at Christmas, I figured it must be him. But if you're not going to marry him, then who is it?' When she didn't answer, but merely stared down at her hands, he said quietly, with sudden enlightenment, 'It's Robichaux, isn't it?'

She hesitated for a long moment, then nodded slowly, 'Yes,' she whispered. 'Naturally, though, I expect you to treat this confidentially.'

'Of course,' he agreed automatically. 'But look here, Autumn, if you love Robichaux, then why leave?'

'A number of reasons,' she said with a wan smile. 'Believe me, Ellis, it's the only thing I can do.'

He shook his head sadly. 'I only wish it were in my power to persuade you to stay.'

She patted his hand. 'So do I,' she agreed. 'I love it here and I'm going to miss it all—and everyone I've met—dreadfully. I've come to look upon this part of the world as my own special place.'

When they reached Bellefleur, Ellis walked her to the door on the shadowy veranda and they stood talking in low murmurs for quite some time, each reluctant to part, knowing that for all intents and purposes, even though they might see each other again during the next two weeks, this was their private goodbye.

At last Autumn made a move to go inside, and Ellis, groaning, pulled her into his arms. 'At least I deserve a goodbye kiss,' he murmured before his lips claimed hers.

As once before, like a bad movie re-run, the porch light flipped on and the front door opened. Autumn tugged her way out of Ellis's embrace and turned to glare at Bill. His face was dark with anger and dislike. 'Sorry,' he said in a chipped voice. 'I was expecting a man who's coming to pick up some medicine. I thought it was him.' With that, he

closed the door and flipped off the light, leaving them standing in thick darkness once more.

'I'd better go inside,' Autumn said shakily. 'Goodnight,
Ellis.'

'Goodbye, Autumn,' he said sadly.

She went inside and turned, on her way upstairs, when
Bill suddenly loomed up from nowhere, blocking her way.
'You're really not particular at all, are you?' he said in a
rude, insolent way.

'W-what do you mean?'

'I mean that you're planning to marry one man but you
have no qualms about kissing another. Easy favours!'

'You're despicable!' she gasped.

He grinned sardonically and his eyes glittered as they
narrowed and studied her. 'Maybe so,' he agreed, 'but I'll
get myself a share of it, too, all the same.' Without any warning, he dissolved the space between them, jerked her into
his arms with an angry, rough gesture and brutally assaulted
her lips. She struggled, but his strong arms kept hers pinned
to her sides, while the kiss went on and on until Autumn
thought her lungs would burst from lack of oxygen. Then
his lips travelled down, down her throat, down to the cleft
between her breasts, turning her bones to water and making
her dizzy and completely limp and totally helpless either to
stop him or to cry out.

Then all at once, he shoved her away, looked long into
her eyes with an unreadable expression in his, then turned
and left her without saying a word.

After that, Autumn saw him only at work. Somehow he
managed always to be out from the house until very late at
night, and the arrangement suited her fine. It was the only
possible way to get through the remaining days and nights
at Bellefleur—if they didn't have to see each other at all
except on a professional basis and with others around.

She would never forgive him for his hateful words and
actions that night, and she knew she had made the right
decision about leaving and going back to New York, despite

objections from friends like Marianne and Grace and
Dianne. And dear Bertha's tearful objections and arguments
didn't bear thinking of. Nevertheless, the sooner she got
entirely away from Bill, the sooner she had at least a fighting
chance of getting over the horrible ache that now resided
permanently in the region of her heart. Anger, hurt and
love all raged inside her like a torrent of water bursting
from a dam. For peace of mind and sanity, it was *imperative*
that she get away. '

But it would be asking too much of her impetuous heart
to forget—or to never look back. That was asking the impossible, and whatever she had ever been in her life,
Autumn had always been a realist. For the rest of her life,
a certain bronze-skinned, coffee-eyed man would always
occupy an important spot in her memory. It would be her
full-time job to remember as seldom as possible.

Mardi Gras—Fat Tuesday—arrived, a cold blustery day
in February with a threat of rain from grey, leaden skies.
Autumn awoke with a heavy heart, a sharp contrast to the
gaily-spirited holiday revellers she would be seeing later
in the day, because she knew this was it—her last day at
Bellefleur, her last day with her friends in St Pierre . . . her
last day ever to see Bill Robichaux. If indeed she were
even to see him at all today. The office would be closed, so
it just might chance that she wouldn't see him even once
more before she left.

But she saw him at once when she arrived at the re-
viewers' stand in front of City Hall before the parade. She
had come with Marianne and, as she climbed the stairs to
the makeshift platform, she saw that among others already
seated were Mayor Les LeCompte and his wife Bonnie, and
beside them were Pauline Blanchard and Bill. A tight vice
squeezed Autumn't heart as she followed Marianne to her
seat on the other side of the Mayor. Now she had the
trying ordeal of smiling brightly and greeting the others as
though this were one of the happiest and most exciting days
of her life.

'Hope you'll like our celebration here,' Les told her. 'We may not be as big or as elaborate as New Orleans, but we certainly have as much fun as they do,' he said with mayoral pride.

'I'm bound to like this better,' Autumn assured him, 'because here I know so many wonderful people. New Orleans might be more glamorous, but it wouldn't be as exciting because they would all be strangers.'

'That's exactly how I feel,' said Bonnie. On the other side of her were Pauline and Bill, who had both ignored Autumn's arrival. Now Autumn faced the street, determined not to let their presence bother her.

Like all parades, this one was late in starting, but at last, around a corner and on to Main Street came two policemen on motorcycles with sirens blowing to warn everyone that the parade was indeed here at last. A great shout of excitement went up from the crowds which lined each side of the street.

Many of the holidaymakers waiting to see the parade were dressed in costumes and masks themselves. There was an entire family of clowns here, a couple of Indians holding hands over there, a large Louisiana crawfish, complete with pinchers, An Alice in Wonderland. She waved to a high school girl she knew from Grace Hebert's class who was today a hobo instead of a very pretty girl. Everyone seemed to be in a rollicking good mood this day before Ash Wednesday and the beginning of Lent.

Now the motorcycles roared past. Next came the Civil Air Patrol bearing the Colours, then the convertible carrying the Past King. More police, in cars now, the High School marching band, the Captain of the Ball and finally, what they had been waiting for, the King's Float, which stopped before the reviewing stand.

Les, as mayor, made a short speech. Then there were champagne toasts from the Mayor to the King and his Queen, from the King to his Queen, from the King to his wife, who beamed proudly as she carried her own glass of champagne to her lips, and many other toasts as well, so that Autumn lost track. But finally the King's float moved on. Then the real madness began, as Dukes from the floats following threw baubles to the screaming, grabbing crowds. 'Throw me a necklace, mister!' 'Hey, throw me a doubloon!' while Marianne explained to Autumn that these inexpensive trinkets were highly prized and people went home from Mardi Gras parades measuring their success by how much loot they had accumulated.

After the parade, Autumn was invited to attend the luncheon for all the Krewe members. She looked for Bill amongst the milling crowd, but he simply wasn't there—which was a bit puzzling to her since Pauline was present.

After the luncheon, she went home to rest for the few remaining hours before the evening festivities. The tableau would be at eight, followed by the ball. Autumn had never felt less like attending a dance in her life. She had refused Ellis's escort, so, in all probability, she would come away shortly after the presentation of the royal Court. If she made an early night, she'd be able to make an early start in the morning.

When she reached the house, Bertha told her that Bill had stopped in for a quick lunch before rushing out again. 'Peoples still get sick,' she said, 'even if it is Carnival. He also left a message for you, *chère*,' she added.

'For me?' Autumn looked at her with startled surprise.

Bertha nodded. 'He said to tell you to be ready for the ball by seven-fifteen. He will take you.'

Autumn was suddenly suffused with different emotions... indignant anger at Bill's high-handed orders, swift joy at the knowledge that if he was planning to take her to the ball it meant he didn't have a date with Pauline, deep unhappiness at the knowledge that in all likelihood this would be their last time ever to see one another, depression that that was probably why he was giving up his evening to be with her and, finally, a certain thrill that wouldn't be ignored, that she could be with him tonight just once more. It was a chance to seize—a chance to memorise his face and his voice and to store them away for all time.

At precisely seven-ten that evening she went downstairs, wearing a golden gown that cast fiery flaming highlights to her hair, which she wore hanging loose and soft around her face. The bodice of the gown gently moulded itself around her breasts before tucking into her small waist and then finally out at the hips to reach the floor in soft folds. The only jewellery she wore was the necklace Bill had given her at Christmas, and now it burned like fire against her bare skin.

Bill was waiting for her at the foot of the stairs and she paused on the last step before reaching the floor. Silently, soberly, they regarded one another, she in her elegant gown, he in his dark evening clothes. His eyes held no glimmer of gladness at seeing her. 'You look . . . incredibly beautiful,' he said at last, as though the words had been dragged out of him.

'Thank you,' she said quietly, as she descended the last step until she stood directly in front of him. Knowing how he felt about her looks, she took no pleasure in his words, but merely responded with an automatic politeness.

'Are you all ready for the excitement of your first Mardi Gras ball?'

'I suppose so,' she answered tonelessly.

'When are you leaving for New York?'

'I plan to make an early start tomorrow morning.'

His dark brows contracted over his eyes. 'You're all packed?'

She nodded. 'I'm all packed.'

'Mr Naquin called me in to see him yesterday,' he told her now. 'He says you've deeded Bellefleur to me.' She nodded agreement but didn't speak. After a moment Bill went on, almost goadingly, as though he were trying to get a spark of some emotion, any emotion, out of her, 'Don't you even *mind* giving it up?'

'Of course I mind,' she told him in a husky voice. She

swallowed hard over the lump in her throat. 'I'll miss Bellefleur very much.'

'But not the man who goes with it?'

Her heart thudded and, for the life of her, she couldn't
think of an answer. Instead she gazed with awful intensity
at a button midway down his shirt front.

Suddenly he was gripping both her arms tightly and giving her a little shake, so that she was forced to look up at
him. 'Tell me you really love this guy you're planning to
marry. Tell me you truly love Prescott!'

She met his gaze boldly, opened her mouth to tell him
just that, but somehow the words simply withered and died
in her throat. Instead she jerked her head to the side so that
she no longer needed to meet those probing eyes.

He released her arms from his painful grip and now he
crossed his arms in front of him. 'I thought not,' he said in
grim satisfaction. 'And I know you don't love Naquin. I
saw him this afternoon—he fell from his horse and broke
his leg.' Before she could even cry out in sympathy for her
friend, he went on, 'I sent him to the hospital. I offered to
fetch you to see him, but he refused. He said he'd asked
you to marry him but you'd turned him down, so there was
no need to call you.' He paused for a moment and instinctively Autumn knew he was trying to get her to look at him.
She was equally determined not to. 'If you're not in love
with this guy in New York, then I'm simply not going to
let you make a huge mistake by going up there and marrying
him.'

'Wh-what do you mean?' she asked breathlessly as she
lifted her eyes at last to look at him.

Bill sighed deeply. 'Look, I know I was hateful to you
the other night, but I promise it won't happen again if you'll
stay. It was just the act of a jealous man. I'm in love with
you, can't you see?'

She just stared at him in blank amazement, unable to
take in the real meaning of what he had just said.

He glared at her angrily. 'Don't look so damned surprised,' he growled at her. 'Surely you could tell that all along?'

She shook her head mutely.

Now his hands had come down to rest on her shoulders again and he was looking into her face with a gentle tenderness she had never seen there before. 'I love you, *chère*,' he said softly. 'So will you please marry me and stay here where people care about you and will treat you well? If you'll only let me show you how much I love you, I'll teach you to love me, too.'

'No,' she whispered hoarsely. 'You could never do that.'

His hands dropped from her shoulders to his sides and the tenderness in his face was displaced by a pain she was well acquainted with. 'I see,' he said stiffly. 'In that case, shall we go now? I'll get your coat.'

He turned from her and took a step away. Autumn, who seemed to have been frozen with shock and disbelief before, now suddenly thawed and moved swiftly. She laid a detaining hand on his dark coat sleeve. 'The reason .. ' Her voice was both husky and shaky and she cleared her throat and tried again. 'The reason you can't ... can't teach me to love you is be-because I already love you, Bill. I've loved you for *such* a long, long time,' she ended with a sigh.

He whirled now and swooped her into his arms in a tight bearlike vice. 'Is that true?' he demanded insistently as his dark eyes smouldered with desire.

She nodded, her eyes shining with her love, and his head bent and his lips claimed hers possessively. Her hands stole up his shoulders, then to his head where her fingers laced themselves through his thick hair. The move incited him so that he crushed her even closer until their two bodies were moulded together.

'Oh, my darling,' he whispered unsteadily at last, 'I've been out of my mind believing you were leaving me—believing you were going to marry that other guy, if not Naquin. I've been crazy with jealousy!'

She laughed shakily. 'I only let you believe I was to save

my pride. Because I thought you were in love with Pauline. I thought you were going to marry her.'

He shook his head and his eyes gazed into hers. 'What I felt for Pauline years ago was a boy's version of love. But then she married someone else and since that I've felt nothing for her at all. Except maybe I was sorry for her when Blanchard died. Plus the fact she has a weak heart. That first night I kissed you ... on the veranda, you remember? ... and she called for me? It was because she was ill.'

Autumn smiled and sighed. 'And I thought you were letting me know that though you might kiss me, your serious interest lay with her,' she confessed.

'We both seem to have got our wires crossed,' he agreed. 'Deliberately or otherwise. But the truth is I've had eyes for no other woman but you ever since that day you looked at me so haughtily and asked me to change your tire.'

'What?' Autumn laughed with disbelief. 'You couldn't have loved me then! You made it too plain you regarded me as a most useless member of society.'

Bill laughed, too, and his voice held a deep timbre of tenderness. 'I have to admit that's what I thought—even though I was falling in love with you against my will. I didn't believe anyone so beautiful could also be such a real, warm person. Until we were stranded at the fishing camp ...' His voice was thick with emotion. 'You were so wonderful then—a real trouper. I almost asked you to marry me then.'

'Oh!' she exclaimed in tearful frustration. 'Why didn't you? Look at all the time we've wasted!'

He shrugged. 'I just thought it was wrong to put you on the spot while we were so isolated, I guess. And once we got back, everything just seemed to start to go wrong for us.' He paused, then asked, 'When was it for you ... knowing you loved me?'

She made a tiny face at him. 'The first time you invited me to New Orleans for the day, when I was committed to spending it with Ellis. You were so angry with me.

'Jealous,' he admitted. 'I was angry again the last time I asked you to New Orleans. That time you didn't even have any prior plans. Why did you turn me down?'

'Because,' she said now, breathlessly shy all at once, 'I was afraid you'd discover my love for you. And only the night before you'd been with Pauline. I was jealous and hurt, too.'

He crushed her to him again. 'I didn't have dinner with Pauline that night, you know,' he confessed. 'But I must admit I hoped you'd think so ... and be jealous!' He bent and kissed the tip of her nose. 'You jumped up and ran out of the office when she was there so fast and so angrily that I finally had a glimmer of hope. But the next day, when you turned me down about New Orleans, I thought I'd been wrong after all.' He paused and gazed at her so lovingly it brought tears to her eyes. 'Marry me soon, darling, I don't think I'll ever believe you really love me until you're really mine.'

'Any time you say,' she told him. 'Bill, I wonder—do you suppose Miss Hattie could have had something like this in mind when she left Bellefleur to me?'

He nodded. 'I was just thinking the same thing, chère. For all she never married herself, she was a great romantic and she was always harping on at me to find a girl to settle down and raise a family with. When you saved her life and proved how brave and compassionate you are as well as beautiful, she must have begun plotting the whole thing out then.'

Autumn's eyes were huge as she looked at him, a bit awed. 'But how could she possibly have known it would work?'

He shook his head. 'She didn't. She merely planted a seed and hoped it would grow. Like a mighty oak.'

Autumn felt a deep gratitude to that kindly little old lady who was surely looking down now from her place among the angels.

'Thanks, Miss Hattie,' she whispered.

'Come on,' said Bill, 'let's go and tell Bertha our news. And then we'll go to the ball and tell all our friends that you're home to stay.'

Bellefleur. What a beautiful name for home!

GREAT LOVE STORIES NEVER GROW OLD...

Like fine old Wedgwood, great love stories are timeless. The pleasure they bring does not decrease through the years. That's why Harlequin is proud to offer...

HARLEQUIN CLASSIC LIBRARY

Delightful old favorites from our early publishing program!

Each volume, first published more than 15 years ago, is an enchanting story of people in love. Each is beautifully bound in an exquisite Wedgwood-look cover. And all have the Harlequin magic, unchanged through the years!

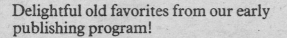

Two **HARLEQUIN CLASSIC LIBRARY** volumes every month! Available NOW wherever Harlequin books are sold.

4 FREE

Harlequin Romances

TAKE THESE 4 FREE

Harlequin Romances

Thrill to romantic, aristocratic Istanbul, and the tender love story of a girl who built a barrier around her emotions in ANNE HAMPSON's "Beyond the Sweet Waters" . . . a Caribbean island is the scene setting for love and conflict in ANNE MATHER's "The Arrogant Duke" . . . exciting, sun-drenched California is the locale for romance and deception in VIOLET WINSPEAR's "Cap Flamingo" . . . and an island near the coast of East Africa spells drama and romance for the heroine in NERINA HILLIARD's "Teachers Must Learn."

Harlequin Romances . . . 6 exciting novels published each month! Each month you will get to know interesting, appealing, true-to-life people . . . . You'll be swept to distant lands you've dreamed of visiting . . . . Intrigue, adventure, romance, and the destiny of many lives will thrill you through each Harlequin Romance novel.

Get all the latest books before they're sold out!

As a Harlequin subscriber you actually receive your personal copies of the latest Romances immediately after they come off the press, so you're sure of getting all 6 each month.

Cancel your subscription whenever you wish!

You don't have to buy any minimum number of books. Whenever you decide to stop your subscription just let us know and we'll cancel all further shipments.